HIS DOG

BY

ALBERT PAYSON TERHUNE

British Library Cataloguing-in-Publication Data
A catalogue record for this book is available from the
British Library

Contents

.

Albert Payson Terhune

Albert Payson Terhune was born on 21st December 1872, in New Jersey, United States. Terhune's father was the Reverend Edward Payson Terhune and his mother, Mary Virginia Hawes, was a writer of household management books and pre-Civil War novels under the name Marion Harland. He was one of six children, having four sisters and one brother, but only two of his sisters survived until adulthood. Further tragedy beset the family when his own wife, Lorraine Bryson Terhune, died four days after giving birth to their only child. He later remarried Anice Terhune, but had no more children.

Terhune received a Bachelor of Arts degree from Columbia University in 1893. The following year, he took a job as a reporter at the New York newspaper The Evening World, a position he held for the next twenty years. During this period, he began to publish works of fiction, such as Dr. Dale: A Story Without A Moral (1900), The New Mayor (1907), Caleb Conover, Railroader (1907), and The Fighter (1909). However, it was his short stories about his collie Lad, published in Red Book, Saturday Evening Post, Ladies' Home Journal, Hartford Courant, and the Atlantic Monthly, that brought him mainstream success. A dozen of these tales were collected into novel form and released as

Lad: A Dog in 1919. This was a best-seller and in 1962 was adapted into a feature film. He went on to produce over thirty novels focusing on the lives of dogs and enjoyed much success in the genre.

Terhune's interest in canines was by no means restricted to fiction. He became a celebrated dog-breeder, specialising in rough collies, lines of which still exist in the breed today. Sunnybank kennels were the most famous collie kennels in the United States and the estate is now open to the public and known as Terhune Memorial Park. Terhune died on 18th February 1942 and was buried at the Pompton Reformed Church in Pompton Lakes, New Jersey.

His Dog

By

Albert Payson Terhune

1922

CHAPTER I.

The Derelict

Link Ferris was a fighter. Not by nature, nor by choice, but to keep alive.

His battleground covered an area of forty acres—broken, scrubby, uncertain side-hill acres, at that. In brief, a worked-out farm among the mountain slopes of the North Jersey hinterland; six miles from the nearest railroad.

The farm was Ferris's, by right of sole heritage from his father, a Civil-War veteran, who had taken up the wilderness land in 1865 and who, for thirty years thereafter, had wrought to make it pay. At best the elder Ferris had wrenched only a meager living from the light and rock-infested soil.

The first-growth timber on the west woodlot for some time had staved off the need of a mortgage; its veteran oaks and hickories grimly giving up their lives, in hundreds, to keep the wolf from the door of their owner. When the last of the salable timber was gone Old Man Ferris tried his hand at truck farming, and sold his wares from a wagon to the denizens of Craigswold, the new colony of rich folk, four miles to northward.

But to raise such vegetables and fruits as would tempt the eyes and the purses of Craigswold people it was necessary to have more than mere zeal and industry. Sour ground will not readily yield sweet abundance, be the toiler ever so industrious. Moreover, there was large and growing competition, in the form of other huckster routes.

And presently the old veteran wearied of the eternal uphill struggle. He mortgaged the farm, dying soon afterward. And Link, his son, was left to carry on the thankless task.

Link Ferris was as much a part of the Ferris farm as was the giant bowlder in the south mowing. He had been born in the paintless shack which his father had built with his own rheumatic hands. He had worked for more than a quarter century, in and out of the hill fields and the ramshackle barns. From babyhood he had toiled there. Scant had been the chances for schooling, and more scant had been the opportunities for outside influence.

Wherefore, Link had grown to a wirily weedy and slouching manhood, almost as ignorant of the world beyond his mountain walls as were any of his own "critters." His life was bounded by fruitless labor, varied only by such sleep and food as might fit him to labor the harder.

He ate and slept, that he might be able to work. And he worked, that he might be able to eat and sleep. Beyond that, his life was as barren as a rainy sea.

If he dreamed of other and wider things, the workaday grind speedily set such dreams to rout. When the gnawing of lonely unrest was too acute for bovine endurance—and when he could spare the time or the money—he was wont to go to the mile-off hamlet of Hampton and there get as nearly drunk as his funds would permit.

It was his only surcease. And as a rule, it was a poor one. For seldom did he have enough ready money to buy wholesale forgetfulness. More often he was able to purchase only enough hard cider or fuseloil whisky to make him dull and vaguely miserable.

It was on his way home one Saturday night from such a rudimentary debauch at Hampton that his Adventure had its small beginning.

For a half mile or so of Link's homeward pilgrimage—before he turned off into the grass-grown, rutted hill trail which led to his farm—his way led along a spur of the state road which linked New York City with the Ramapo hill country.

And here, as Link swung glumly along through the springtide dusk, his ears were assailed by a sound that was something between a sigh and a sob—a sound as of one who tries valiantly to stifle a whimper of sharp pain.

Ferris halted, uncertain, at the road edge; and peered about him. Again he heard the sound. And this time he located it in the long grass of the wayside ditch. The grass was stirring spasmodically, too, as with the half-restrained writhings of something lying close to earth there.

Link struck a match. Shielding the flame, he pushed the tangle of grass to one side with his foot.

There, exposed in the narrow space thus cleared and by the narrower radius of match flare, crouched a dog.

The brute was huddled in a crumpled heap, with one foreleg stuck awkwardly out in front of him at an impossible angle. His tawny mass of coat was mired and oil streaked. In his deep-set brown eyes burned the fires of agony.

Yet, as he looked up at the man who bent above him, the dog's gaze was neither fierce nor cringing. It held rather such an expression as, Dumas tells us, the wounded Athos turned to D'Artagnan—the aspect of one in sore need of aid, and too proud to plead for it.

Link Ferris had never heard of Dumas, nor of the immortal musketeer. None the less, he could read that look. And it appealed to him, as no howl of anguish could have appealed. He knelt beside the suffering dog and fell to examining his hurts.

The dog was a collie—beautiful of head, sweepingly graceful of line, powerful and heavy coated. The mud on his expanse of snowy chest frill and the grease on his dark brown back were easy to account for, even to Link Ferris's none-too-keen imagination.

Link, in his own occasional trudges along this bit of state road, had often seen costly dogs in the tonneaus of passing cars. He had seen several of them scramble frantically to maintain their footing on the slippery seats of such cars; when chauffeurs took the sharp curve, just ahead, at too high

8

speed. He had even seen one Airedale flung bodily from a car's rear seat at that curve, and out into the roadway; where a close-following motor had run over and killed it.

This collie, doubtless, had had such a fall; and, unseen by the front seat's occupants, had struck ground with terrific force—a force that had sent him whirling through mud and grease into the ditch, with a broken front leg.

How long the beast had lain there Link had no way of guessing. But the dog was in mortal agony. And the kindest thing to do was to put him out of his pain.

Ferris groped around through the gloom until, in the ditch, his fingers closed over a ten-pound stone. One smashing blow on the head, with this missile, would bring a swift and merciful end to the sufferer's troubles.

Poising the stone aloft, Link turned back to where the dog lay. Standing over the victim, he balanced the rock and tensed his muscles for the blow. The match had long since gone out, but Link's dusk-accustomed vision could readily discern the outlines of the collie. And he made ready to strike.

Then—perhaps it was the drink playing tricks with Ferris's mind—it seemed to him that he could still see those deep-set dark eyes staring up at him through the murk, with that same fearless and yet piteous look in their depths. It was a look that the brief sputter of match-light had photographed on Link's brain.

"I—I ain't got the heart to swat you while you keep lookin' that way at me," he muttered half-aloud, as if to a human companion. "Jes' you turn your head the other way, pup! It'll be over quick, an' easy."

By the faint light Link could see the dog had not obeyed the order to turn his head. But at the man's tone of compassion the great plumy tail began to thump the ground in feeble response.

"H'm!" grunted Link, letting the stone drop to the road, "got nerve, too, ain't you, friend? 'Tain't every cuss that can wag his tail when his leg's bust."

Kneeling down again he examined the broken foreleg more carefully. Gentle as was his touch, yet Link knew it must cause infinite torture. But the dog did not flinch. He seemed to understand that Ferris meant kindly, for he moved his magnificent head far enough to lick the man's hand softly and in gratitude.

The caress had an odd effect on the loveless Ferris. It was the first voluntary mark of affection he had encountered for longer than he liked to remember. It set old memories to working.

The Ferris farm, since Link's birth, had been perhaps the only home in all that wild region which did not boast a dog of some kind. Link's father had had an inborn hatred of dogs. He would not allow one on the place. His overt excuse was that they killed sheep and worried cattle, and that he could not afford to risk the well-being of his scanty hoard of stock.

Thus, Link had grown to manhood with no dog at his heels, and without knowing the normal human's love for canine chumship.

The primal instinct, long buried, stirred within him now; at touch of the warm tongue on his calloused hand and at sound of that friendly tail wagging in the dry grass. Ashamed of the stirrings in him, he sought to explain them by reminding himself that this was probably a valuable animal and that a reward might be offered for his return. In which case Link Ferris might as well profit by the cash windfall as anyone else.

Taking off his coat, Ferris spread it on the ground. Then, lifting the stricken collie as gently as he could, he deposited him on the coat and rolled its frayed edges about him. After which he picked up the swathed invalid and bore him home.

During the mile trudge the collie's sixty pounds grew unbearably heavy, to the half-drunk Ferris. More than once he was minded to set down his burden and leave the brute to his fate.

But always the tardy realization that the journey was more painful to the dog than to himself gave Link a fresh grip on his determination. And at last,—a long and tiring last,—they reached the tumble-down farmhouse where Link Ferris kept bachelor's hall.

Laying his patient on the kitchen table, Link lighted a candle and went in search of such rude appliances as his father had been wont to keep in store for any of the farm's animals that might be injured.

Three times as a lad Link had seen his father set the broken leg of a sheep, and once he had watched the older man perform a like office for a yearling heifer whose hind leg had become wedged between two brookside stones and had sustained a compound fracture. From Civil War hospital experience the father had been a deft bonesetter. And following his recollection of the old man's methods, Link himself had later set the broken leg of one of his lambs. The operation had been a success. He resolved now to duplicate it.

Slowly and somewhat clumsily he went to work at the injured dog. The collie's brave patience nerved him to greater tenderness and care. A veterinary would have made neater work of the bonesetting, but hardly could have rendered the job more effective.

When the task was achieved Link brought his patient a bowl of cold water—which the collie drank greedily—and some bread and meat scraps which the feverish patient would not touch.

As he worked at his bonesetting task, Ferris had more chance to study his new acquisition. The dog was young—probably not more than two years old. The teeth proved that. He wore a thin collie collar with no inscription on its silver band.

Even to Link's inexperienced eye he was an animal of high breeding and of glorious beauty. Link told himself he would perhaps get as much as ten dollars for the return of so costly a pet. And he wondered why the golden prospect did not seem more alluring.

Three times in the night Link got up to give the collie fresh water and to moisten and re-adjust the bandages. And, every time, the sight of his rescuer would cause the dog's tail to thump a joyous welcome and would fill the dark eyes with a loving gratitude which went straight to Ferris's lonely heart.

In the morning the dog was prevailed upon to lap a saucer of warm milk, and even to nibble at a crust of soaked bread. Link was ashamed of his own keen and growing interest in his find. For the first time he realized how bleakly lonesome had been his home life, since the death of his father had left him solitary.

There was a mysteriously comforting companionship in the dog's presence. Link found himself talking to him from time to time as to a fellow human. And the words did not echo back in eerie hollowness from the walls, as when he had sometimes sought to ease his desolation by talking aloud to himself.

He was embarrassed by his general ignorance of dogs, and by his ignorance of this particular dog's name. He sought to learn what the collie had been called; by trying one familiar dog name after another. But, to such stand-by cognomens as Rover, Tige, Fido, Ponto, Shep and the rest, the patient gave no further sign of recognition than a friendly wagging of his plumed tail. And he wagged it no more interestedly for one name than for another.

So Ferris ceased from the effort, and decided to give his pet a brand-new name for such brief space as they should be housemates. After long deliberation he hit upon the name "Chum," as typical of the odd friendship that was springing to life between the dog and himself. And he planned to devote much time to teaching the collie this name.

But, to his surprise, no such tedious period of instruction was necessary. In less than a single day Chum knew his name,—knew it past all doubt.

Link was amazed at such cleverness. For three solid months, at one time, he had striven to teach his horse and his cows and a few of his sheep to respond to given names. And at the end of the course of patient tutelage he had been morbidly certain that not one of his solemn-eyed pupils had grasped the lessons.

It was surprisingly pleasant to drop in at the kitchen door nowadays, in intervals between chores or at the day's end, and be greeted by that glad glint of the eye and the ecstatic pounding of the wavy tail against the floor. It was still pleasanter to see the gaze of wistful adoration that strengthened daily as Chum and his new master grew better and better acquainted.

Pleasantest of all was it to sit and talk to the collie in the once-tedious evenings, and to know that his every word was appreciated and listened to with eager interest, even if the full gist of the talk itself did not penetrate to the listener's understanding.

Link Ferris, for the first time in his life, had a dog. Incidentally, for the first time in his life, he had an intimate friend—something of whose love and loyalty he waxed increasingly sure. And he was happy.

His brighter spirits manifested themselves in his farm work, transforming drudgery into contentment. And the farm began, in small ways, to show the effects of its owner's new attitude toward labor.

The day after he found Chum, Link had trudged to Hampton; and, there, had affixed to the clapboards of the general store a bit of paper whereon he had scrawled:

"Found-One white and brown bird dog with leg broken. Owner can have same by paying a reward."

On his next huckster trip to Craigswold he pinned a similar sign to the bulletin board of that rarefied resort's post-office. And he waited for results.

He did more. He bought two successive copies of the county's daily paper and scanned it for word of a missing dog. But in neither copy did he find what he sought.

True, both editions carried display advertisements which offered a seventy-five dollar reward for information leading to the return of a "dark-sable-and-white collie lost somewhere between Hohokus and Suffern."

The first time he saw this notice Link was vaguely troubled lest it might refer to Chum. He told himself he hoped it did. For seventy-five dollars just now would be a godsend. And in self-disgust he choked back a most annoying twinge of grief at thought of parting with the dog.

Two things in the advertisement puzzled him. In the first place, as Chum was longhaired and graceful, Link had mentally classified him as belonging to the same breed as did the setters which accompanied hunters on mountain rambles past his farm in the autumns. Being wholly unversed in canine lore, he had, therefore, classified Chum as a "bird dog". The word "collie", if ever he had chanced to hear it before, carried no meaning to him.

Moreover, he did not know what "sable" meant. He asked Dominie Jansen, whom he met on the way home. And the dominie told him "sable" was another name for "black."

Jansen went on to amplify the theme, dictionary-fashion, by quoting a piece of sacred poetry about "the sable wings of night."

A great load was off Link's heart. Chum, most assuredly, was not black and white. So the advertisement could not possibly refer to him. The reverend gentleman, not being a dog fancier, of course had no means of knowing that "sable", in collie jargon, means practically every shade of color except black or gray or white.

Link was ashamed of his own delight in finding he need not give up his pet—even for seventy-five dollars. He tried to recall his father's invectives against dogs, and to remind himself that another mouth to feed on the farm must mean still sharper poverty and skimping. But logic could not strangle joy, and life took on a new zest for the lonely man.

By the time Chum could limp around on the fasthealing foreleg, he and Link had established a friendship that was a boon to both and a stark astonishment to Ferris.

Link had always loved animals. He had an inborn "way" with them. Yet his own intelligence had long since taught him that his "farm critters" responded but dully to his attempts at a more perfect understanding.

He knew, for example, that the horse he had bred and reared and had taught to come at his call, would doubtless suffer the first passing stranger to mount him and ride him away, despite any call from his lifelong master. He knew that his presence, to the cattle and sheep, meant only food or a shift of quarters; and that an outsider could drive or tend them as readily as could he on whose farm they had been born. Their possible affection for him was a hazy thing, based solely on what he fed them and on their occasional mild interest in being petted.

But with Chum it was all different. The dog learned quickly his new master's moods and met them in kind. The few simple tricks Link sought to teach him were grasped with bewildering ease. There was a human quality of sympathy and companionship which radiated almost visibly from Chum. His keen collie brain was forever amazing Ferris by its flashes of perception. The dog was a revelation and an endless source of pleasure to the hermit-farmer.

When Chum was whole of his hurt and when the injured leg had knit so firmly that the last trace of lameness was gone, Link fell to recalling his father's preachments as to the havoc wrought by dogs upon sheep. He could not afford to lose the leanest and toughest of his little sheep flock—even as price for the happiness of owning a comrade. Link puzzled sorely over this.

Then one morning it occurred to him to put the matter up to Chum himself. Hitherto he had kept the dog around the house, except on their daily walks; and he had always tied him when driving the sheep to or from pasture. This morning he took the collie along when he went out to release the tiny flock from their barnyard fold and send them out to graze.

Link opened the fold gate, one hand on Chum's collar. Out billowed the sheep in a ragged scramble. Chum quivered with excitement as the woolly catapults surged past him. Eagerly he looked up into his master's face, then back at the tumbling creatures.

"Chum!" spoke Ferris sharply. "Leave 'em be! Get that? LEAVE 'EM BE!"

He tightened his hold on the collar as he gave the command. Chum ceased to quiver in eagerness and stood still, half puzzled, half grieved by the man's unwonted tone.

The sheep, at sight and smell of the dog, rushed jostlingly from their pen and scattered in every direction, through barnyard and garden and nearer fields. Bleating and stampeding, they ran. Link Ferris blinked after them, and broke into speech. Loudly and luridly he swore.

This stampede might well mean an hour's running to and fro before the scattered flock could be herded once more. An hour of panting and blasphemous pursuit, at the very outset of an overbusy day. And all because of one worthless dog.

His father had been right. Link saw that—now that it was too late. A dog had no place on a farm. A poor man could not afford the silly luxury of a useless pet. With whistle and call Ferris sought to check the flight of the flock. But, as every farmer knows, there is nothing else on earth quite so unreasonable and idiotic as a scared sheep. The familiar summons did not slacken nor swerve the stampede.

The fact that this man had been their protector and friend made no difference to the idiotic sheep. They were frightened. And, therefore, the tenuously thin connecting line between them and their human master had snapped. For the moment they were merely wild animals, and he was a member of a hostile race—almost as much as was the huge dog that had caused their fright.

A wistful whine from Chum interrupted Link's volley of swearing. The dog had noted his master's angry excitement and was seeking to offer sympathy or help.

But the reminder of Chum's presence did not check Link's wrath at the unconscious cause of the stampede. He loosed his hold on the collar, resolving to take out his rage in an unmerciful beating should the dog seek to chase the fleeing sheep. That would be at least an outlet for the impotent wrath which Ferris sought to wreak on someone or something.

"Go get 'em then, if you're so set on it!" he howled at the collie, waving a windmill arm at the fugitives. "Only I'll whale your measly head off if you do!"

The invitation and the gesture that went with it seemed to rouse some long-dormant memory in the collie's soul. Like a flash he was off in flying pursuit of the sheep. Ferris, in the crazy rage which possessed him, hoped Chum might bite at least one of the senseless creatures that were causing him such a waste of precious time and of grudged effort.

Wherefore he did not call back the fastrunning collie. It would be time enough to whale the daylight out of him— yes, and to rescue his possible victims from death—when the dog should have overhauled the woolly pests. So, in dour fury, Link watched the pursuit and the flight.

Then, of a sudden, the black rage in Ferris's visage changed to perplexity, and slowly from that to crass wonderment.

Six of the sheep had remained bunched in their runaway dash, while all the rest had scattered singly. It was after this bleating sextet that Chum was now racing.

Nor did he stop when he came up with them. Tearing past them he wheeled almost in midair and slackened his pace, running transversely ahead of them and breaking into a clamor of barks.

The six, seeing their foe menacing them from in front, came to a jumbled and slithering halt, preparing to break their formation and to scatter. But Chum would not have it so.

Still threatening them with his thunderous bark he made little dashes at one or another of them that tried to break away; and he crowded back the rest.

As a result, there was but one direction the dazed sheep could take—the direction whence they had come. And, uncertainly, shamblingly, they made their way back toward the fold.

Scarce had they been fairly started in their cowed progress when Chum was off at a tangent, deserting his six charges and bearing down with express train speed on a stray wether that had paused in his escape to nibble at a line of early peas in the truck garden.

At sight of the approaching collie the sheep flung up its head and began again to run. But the dog was in front of it, whichever way the panic-stricken animal turned;—in every direction but one. And in that direction fled the fugitive. Nor did it stop in its headlong flight until it was alongside the six which Chum had first "turned".

Pausing only long enough to round up one or two sheep which were breaking loose from the bunch Chum was off again in headlong chase of still another and another and another stray.

Link Ferris, in blank incredulity, stood gaping at the picture before him—staring at the tireless swiftness of his dog in turning back and rounding up a scattered flock which Ferris himself could not have bunched in twenty times the space of minutes. Chum, he noted, did not touch one of the foolish beasts. His bark and his zigzag dashes served the purpose, without the aid of teeth or of actual contact.

Presently, as the dumbfounded man gazed, the last stray was added to the milling, bleating bunch, and Chum was serenely trotting to and fro, driving back such of the sheep as sought to break loose from the huddle. Terrified and trembling, but mastered, the flock cowered motionless. The work was done.

As in a dream Link tumbled toward the prisoners. His mind functioning subconsciously, he took up his interrupted task of driving them to pasture. The moment he succeeded in getting them into motion they broke again. And again, like a furry whirlwind, Chum was encircling them; chasing the strays into place. He saw, without being told, the course his master was taking, and he drove his charges accordingly.

Thus, in far less time and in better order than ever before, the flock reached the rickety gateway of the stone-strewn sheep pasture and scuttled jostlingly in through it.

Link shut the gate after them. Then, still in a daze, he turned on the dog.

"Chum," he said confusedly, "it don't make sense to me, not even yet. I don't get the hang of it. But I know this much: I know you got ten times the sense what I'VE got. Where you got it an' how you got it the good Lord only knows. But you've got it. I—I was figgerin' on lickin' you 'most to death, a few minutes back. Chum. Honest, I was. I'm clean 'shamed to look you in the face when I think of it. Say! Do me a favor, Chum. If ever I lift hand to lick you, jes' bite me and give me hydrophoby. For I'll sure be deservin' it. Now come on home!"

He patted the silken head of the jubilant dog as he talked, rumpling the soft ears and stroking the long, blazed muzzle. He was sick at heart at memory of his recent murderous rage at this wonder-comrade of his.

Chum was exultantly happy. He had had a most exhilarating ten minutes. The jolliest bit of fun he could remember in all his two years of life. The sight of those queer sheep—yes, and the scent of them, especially the scent—had done queer things to his brain; had aroused a million sleeping ancestral memories.

He had understood perfectly well his master's order that he leave them alone. And he had been disappointed by it. He himself had not known clearly what it was he would have liked to do to them. But he had known he and they ought to have some sort of relationship. And then at the gesture and the snarled command of "Go get them!" some closed door in Chum's mind had swung wide, and, acting on an instinct he himself did not understand, he had hurled himself into the gay task of rounding up the flock.

So, for a thousand generations on the Scottish hills, had Chum's ancestors earned their right to live. And so through successive generations had they imbued their progeny with that accomplishment until it had become a primal instinct. Even as the unbroken pointer of the best type knows by instinct the rudiments of his work in the field so will many a collie take up sheep herding by ancestral training.

There had been nothing wonderful in Chum's exploit. Hundreds of untrained collies have done the same thing on their first sight of sheep. The craving to chase and slay sheep is a mere perversion of this olden instinct; just as the disorderly "flushing" and scattering of bird coveys is a perversion of the pointer or setter instinct. Chum, luckily for himself and for his master's flock, chanced to run true to form in this matter of heredity, instead of inheriting his tendency in the form of a taste for sheep murder.

The first collie, back in prehistoric days, was the first dog with the wit to know his master's sheep apart from all other sheep. Perhaps that is the best, if least scientific, theory of the collie's origin.

But to Link Ferris's unsophisticated eyes the achievement was all but supernatural, and it doubled his love for the dog.

That afternoon, by way of experiment, Ferris took Chum along when he went to drive the sheep back from pasture to the fold. By the time he and the dog were within a hundred yards of the pasture gate Chum began to dance, from sheer anticipation; mincing sidewise on the tips of his toes in true collie fashion, and varying the dance by little rushes forward.

Link opened the crazy gate. Waiting for no further encouragement the dog sped into the broad field and among the grazing sheep that were distributed unevenly over the entire area of the lot.

Ordinarily—unless the sheep were ready to come home—it was a matter of ten or fifteen minutes each evening for Link to collect them and start them on their way. To-day, in less than three minutes, Chum had the whole flock herded and trotting through the opening, to the lane outside.

Nor, this time, did the sheep flee from him in the same panic dread as in the morning. They seemed to have learned—if indeed a sheep can ever learn anything—that Chum was their driver, not their enemy.

From the fold Link as usual went to the woodlot where his five head of lean milch cattle were at graze. Three of the cows were waiting at the bars for him, but one heifer and a new-dry Holstein were hidden somewhere in the recesses of the second-growth timber.

The afternoon was hot; it had been a hot day. Link was tired. He dreaded the labor of exploring ten acres of undergrowth for his two missing cattle. An inspiration came to him. Pointing to the three stolidly waiting cows at the bars he waved his arm in the general direction of the lot and called on Chum.

"Go find 'em! Bring 'em in!"

Almost before the words were spoken Ferris regretted them. He hated to dim the luster of his dog's earlier exploits by giving him a job beyond his skill. And this time Chum did not flash forward with his former zest. He stood, ears cocked, glancing uncertainly from Link to the three cows already waiting.

Then, as he still peered doubtfully, one of the bovine trio took fright at the dog and trotted clumsily away toward the woods. Link gave chase. He had not gone three steps before Chum caught the idea. Whirling past Ferris he headed off the surprised, indignant cow, and by dint of a flurry of barks and dashes started her back toward the bars.

Her bell jangled dolefully as she obeyed the noisy urge. And from somewhere among the bushes, two hundred yards away, a second cowbell sounded in answer. At this distant tinkle Chum evidently grasped the meaning of his master's earlier mandate. For he galloped away in the direction of the sound.

And presently, with much crashing of undergrowth, appeared the rebellious heifer, driven on by Chum. After depositing her, sulky and plunging, at the bars, Chum vanished again—in apparent response to another far-off bell jangle. And in three minutes more he was back at the bars with the fifth cow.

"Lucky one was a heifer an' the other one dry!" commented Link to the collie, after petting him and praising him for the exploit. "I'll have to learn you to drive milch cows easy an' quiet. You can't run 'em like you run sheep an' yearlin's. But apart from that, you sure done grand. You can lop off an hour a day of my work if I c'n send you reg'lar for the critters. That ought to be worth the price of your keep, by itself. Now if I c'n learn you how to milk an' maybe how to mow—well, 'twouldn't be a hull lot queerer'n the stunts you done to-day!"

It was perhaps a week later that Link Ferris received his quarterly check from the Paterson Vegetable Market. These checks hitherto had been the brightest spots in Link's routine. Not only did the money for his hard-raised farm products mean a replenishing of the always scant larder and an easing of the chronic fiscal strain between himself and the Hampton general store's proprietor, but sometimes enough spare cash was left over to allow Ferris to get very satisfactorily drunk.

Since Chum's advent, the old gnawing of loneliness had not goaded Link to the Hampton tavern. As a consequence, he had a dollar or two more on hand than was usual at such times. This wealth was swelled still further by the fact that a boost in vegetable prices had fattened his quarterly check beyond its wonted size.

All this and his long abstinence seemed to call for a real celebration. And Link looked forward with a thrill of merry anticipation to the coming of night.

As soon as he could clear away his evening chores and swallow some supper he fared forth to the village. This was going to be one of those nights to date time from. Not a miserable half-jag, stopped in mid-career by lack of funds and of credit—a nipped-in-the-bud debauch, such as so often had sent him home cranky and unsatisfied and railing against poverty. No, this was going to be the real thing—a record performance, even for these pre-prohibition times.

Ferris fed the collie and shut him into the kitchen, pending his own return from Hampton. If Link were going to become blissfully and helplessly drunk, as he had every hope of being, someone might take advantage of his condition to steal his precious dog. Therefore Chum was best left safe at home. This Link explained very carefully to the interestedly listening collie. And Chum, with head and brush a-droop, walked meekly into the kitchen at his master's behest.

Link set off for the village, happy in the feeling that his home was so well guarded and that he would find a loving friend waiting to welcome him on his return. What with ready money and a real friend and the prospect of getting whole-souledly drunk the world was not such a rotten place to live in after all!

As a rule, on these occasions, Ferris first went to the Hampton store. There he was wont to cash his check, pay his longstanding bill, order his new supplies—and then, with a free heart, sally forth to the Hampton tavern. But to-night, having money in his pocket apart from the check, he decided to pay a preliminary call at the tavern, just by way of warming up, before going on to the store.

There were few people in the barroom at so early an hour of the evening and on so early an evening of the week. Link nodded affably to one or two men he knew and bade them line up at the bar with him. After the second drink he prepared to leave. To the tavern's proprietor, who was mildly surprised at the brevity of his call, Ferris explained that he was going across to the store to get his check cashed and that he would be back later.

Whereat the proprietor kindly offered to save Link the journey by cashing the check for him; a suggestion Ferris gladly accepted. He passed the indorsed check across the bar and received for it a comfortably large wad of wilted greenbacks which he proceeded to intern with tender care in an inside pocket of his vest, where he moored them with a safety-pin. Then he ordered another drink.

But to this new order there was an instant demurrer. Two strangers, who had been drinking at a corner table, bore down upon Link right lovingly; and recalled themselves to his memory as companions of his on a quite forgotten debauch of a year or two back.

Link did not at all remember either of the two. But then he often failed to recall people he had met on a spree, and he did not like to hurt these cordial revelers' feelings by disclaiming knowledge of them. Especially when they told him merrily that, for this evening at least, his money was made of wood and that he must be their guest.

Never before had he met with such wholesouled hospitality. One drink followed another with gratifying speed. Once or twice Ferris made halfhearted proffers to do some of the buying. But such hints seemed to hurt his hosts' feelings so cruelly that he forbore at last, and suffered himself to drink entirely at their expense.

They were much the nicest men Link had ever met. They flattered him. They laughed uproariously at his every witticism. They had a genius for noting when his glass was empty. They listened with astonished admiration to his boastful recital of Chum's cleverness. One of them, who, it seemed, was an expert in dog lore, told him how to teach the collie to shake hands and to lie down and to "speak." They were magnificent men, in every way. Link was ashamed to have forgotten his earlier meetings with such paragons.

But the call of duty never quite dies into silence. And finally Link remembered he had still his store bill to pay and his supplies to order. So he announced that he must go. The store, he knew, closed at nine. He looked up at the barroom clock. But its face was hazy and it seemed to have a great many hands. There was no use trying to learn the hour from so dissolute a timepiece.

His two friends persuaded him to have one more drink. Then they volunteered to go across to the store with him. He left the tavern, with one of the two walking on either side of him. He was glad to be in the center of the trio; for, as the night air struck him, he became unaccountably dizzy. His friends' willing arms were a grand support to his wavering legs.

On the unlighted threshold of the tavern Link stumbled heavily over something—something that had been lying there and that sprang eagerly toward him as he debouched from the doorway. The reason he stumbled over it was that the creature, which had bounded so rapturously toward him, had come to a sharp halt at noting his condition. Thus, Ferris stumbled over it; and would have fallen but for the aid of his friends.

The single village street was pitch black. Not a light was to be seen. This puzzled Link; who had no means of knowing that the time was close on midnight. He started toward the store. At least that was the direction he planned to take. But when, at the end of five minutes, he found he was outside the village and on a narrow road that bordered the lake, he saw his friends had mistaken the way. He stopped abruptly and told them so.

One of them laughed; as if Link had said something funny. The other did something quickly with one foot and one arm. Ferris's legs went from under him. The jar of his fall

32

shook from him a fraction of his drunkenness, and it gave him enough sense to realize that the man who had laughed was trying to unfasten the pinned inner pocket of the fallen man's vest.

Now for years that pocket had been the secret repository of Link Ferris's sparse wealth. The intruder's touch awakened him to a drowsy sense of peril. He thrust aside the fumbling hand and made a herculean effort to rise.

At this show of resistance his two comrades, as by concerted signal, threw themselves upon him. With a yell of angry fright Link collapsed to earth under the dual impact.

CHAPTER II.

The Battle

He felt one of the men pinion his waving arms, while the other crouched on his legs and proceeded to unpin the money pocket. Ferris struggled for an instant in futile fury, trying to shout for help. The call was strangled in his throat. But the help came to him, none the less.

Scarce three seconds had passed since the attempt to rob him had set Link into action and had wrung from him that yell of consternation.

But in answer came a swirling patter of feet on the road, a snarl like a wolf's, a shape that catapulted through the dark. Sixty pounds of fur-swathed dynamic muscle smote athwart the shoulders of the man who was unfastening the cash pocket's pin.

The impact hurled the fellow clean off his crouching balance and sent him sprawling, face downward, his outflung hands splashing in the margin of the lake. Before he could roll over or so much as stir, a set of white fangs met in his shoulder-flesh. And he testified to his injury by an eldritch screech of pain and terror that echoed far across the water.

His companion, rallying from the momentary shock, left Ferris and charged at the prostrate thief's assailant. But

Chum met him, with a fierce eagerness, more than half way.

A true collie—thanks to his strain of wolf bloodfights as does no other dog. What he lacks in stubborn determination he atones for by swiftness and by his uncanny brain power.

A bulldog, for example, would have flown to his master's relief quite as readily as did Chum. But a bulldog would have secured the first convenient hold and would have hung on to that hold, whether it were at his victim's throat or only on the slack of his trousers—until someone should hammer him into senselessness.

Chum—collie-fashion—was everywhere at once, using his brain far more than his flying jaws. Finding the grip in his foe's shoulder did not prevent the man from twisting round to grapple him, the collie shifted that grip with lightning speed, and with one of his gleaming eyeteeth slashed his opponent's halfturned cheek from eye to chin. Then he bored straight for the jugular.

It was at this crisis that he sensed, rather than saw, the other man rushing at him. Chum left his fallen antagonist and whirled about to face the new enemy. As he was still turning, he sprang far to one side, in bare time to elude a swinging kick aimed at his head.

Then, before the thief could recover the balance endangered by so mighty a kick, the collie had whirled in and sunk his teeth deep in the man's calf. The bitten man let out a roar of pain, and smote wildly at the dog's face with both swinging fists.

Chum leaped back out of range, and then, with the same bewildering speed, flashed in again and buried his curved fangs in the nearest of the two flailing forearms.

The first victim of the collie's attack was scrambling to his feet. So was Link Ferris. Sobered enough to recognize his beloved dog, he also saw the newrisen thief catch up a broken fence rail, brandish it aloft and charge upon the collie, who was still battling merrily with the second man.

To Link it seemed that nothing could save Chum from a backbreaking blow from the huge club. Instinctively he ran at the wielder of the formidable weapon. Staggering and sick and two-thirds drunk, Ferris, nevertheless, made valiant effort to save the dog that was fighting so gallantly for him.

His lurching rush carried him across the narrow road and to the lake edge, barely in time to intercept the swinging sweep of the fence rail. It caught him glancingly across the side. And its force carried him clean off his none-too-steady feet. Down went Ferris—down and backward. His body plunged noisily into the water.

Chum had wheeled to face the rail's brandisher. But at sight of his master's sudden immersion in the lake, he quitted the fray. At top speed the dog cleared the bank and jumped down into the water in pursuit of Ferris.

It evidently dawned on both men at once that there had been a good deal of noise, for what was to have been a silent and decorous holdup. Also that a raging collie is not a pleasant foe. The racket might well draw interference from outside. The dog was overhard to kill, and his bites were murderous. The game had ceased to be worth the candle. By common impulse the pair took to their heels.

Link Ferris, head down in the cold water, was strangling in his maudlin efforts to right himself. He dug both hands into the lake-bottom mud and strove to gain the surface. But the effort was too much for him. A second frantic heave had better results. And vaguely he knew why.

For Chum had managed to get a firm hold on the shoulder of his master's coat—twelve inches under water—and had braced himself with all his wiry strength for a tug which should lift Ferris to the surface.

This added leverage barely made Link's own struggle a success. The half-drowned man regained his footing. Floundering waist-deep in water, he clambered up the steeply shelving bank to shore. There at the road's edge he lay, gasping and sputtering and fighting for breath.

Chum had been pulled under and out of his depth by Link's exertions. Now, coming to the surface, he swam to shore and trotted up the bank to the road. Absurdly lank and small, with his soaking coat plastered close to his slim body, he stood over his prostrate master.

The dog's quick glare up and down the road told him his foes were gone. His incredible sense of hearing registered the far-off pad-pad-pad of fast-retreating human feet, and showed him the course the two men were taking. He would have liked to give chase. It had been a good fight—lively and exciting withal—and Chum wished he might carry it into the enemies' own country.

But his god was lying helpless at his feet and making queer sounds of distress. The dog's place was here. The joy of battle must be foregone.

Solicitously Chum leaned over Ferris and sought to lick the sufferer's face. As he did so his supersensitive nostrils were smitten by an odor which caused the collie to shrink back in visible disgust. The sickly, pungent smell of whisky on Ferris's labored breath nauseated Chum. He stood, head recoiled, looking down at Link in bewilderment.

There were many things, this night, which Chum did not understand. First of all, he had been grieved and offended that Ferris should have locked him in the kitchen instead of taking him along as usual on his evening stroll. It had been lonely in the unlighted kitchen. Link had not ordered the dog to stay there. He had simply shut Chum in and left him.

So, tiring at last of solitude, the collie had leaped lightly out of the nearest window. The window had been open. Its thin mosquito net covering had not served in the least as a deterrent to the departing Chum.

To pick up his master's trail—and to hold to it even when it merged with a score of others at the edge of the village—had been absurdly simple. The trail had led to a house with closed doors. So, after circling the tavern to find if his master had gone out by any other exit, Chum had curled himself patiently on the doorstep and had waited for Link to emerge.

Several people had come in and out while he lay there. But all of them had shut the door too soon for him to slip inside.

At last Ferris had appeared between his two new friends. Chum had been friskily happy to see his long-absent god again. He had sprung forward to greet Link. Then, his odd collie sense had told him that for some reason this staggering and hiccuping creature was not the master whom he knew and loved. This man was strangely different from the Link Ferris whom Chum knew.

Puzzled, the dog had halted and had stood irresolute. As he stood there, Ferris had stumbled heavily over him, hurting the collie's ribs and his tender flesh; and had meandered on without so much as a word or a look for his pet.

Chum, still irresolute and bewildered, had followed at a distance the swaying progress of the trio, until Link's yell and the attack had brought him in furious haste to Ferris's rescue.

Link presently recovered enough of his breath to enable him to move. The ducking in icy water had cleared his bemused brain. Approximately sober, he got to his feet and stood swaying and dazed. As he rose, his groping hand closed over something cold and hard that had fallen to the ground beside him. And he recognized it. So he picked it up and stuck it into his pocket.

It was a pint flask of whisky—one he had received as a farewell gift from his two friends as the three had left the tavern. It had been an easy gift for the men to make. For they were confidently certain of recovering it a few minutes later when they should go through their victim's clothes. Dawning intelligence told Link he had not come through the adventure very badly, after all—thanks to Chum. Ferris well understood now why the thieves had picked acquaintance with him at sight of his money, and why they had gotten him drunk.

The memory of what he had escaped gave him a new qualm of nausea. The loss of his cash would have meant suspended credit at the store and the leanest three months he had ever known.

But soon the joy in his triumph wiped out this thought.

The native North Jersey mountaineer has a peculiar vein of cunning which makes him morbidly eager to get the best of anyone at all—even if the victory brings him nothing worth while.

Link Ferris had had an evening of limitless liquor. He still had a pint of whisky to take home. And it had cost him not a cent, except for his first two rounds of drinks.

He had had his spree. He still had all his check money. And he had a flask of whisky. True, he had been roughly handled. And he had had a ducking in the lake. But those were his sole liabilities. They were insignificant by comparison to his assets.

He grinned in smug self-gratulation. Then his eye fell on Chum, standing ten feet away, looking uncertainly at him.

Chum! To Chum he owed it all! He owed the dog his money, perhaps his very life. Yes—as he rehearsed the struggle to get out of the lake—he owed the collie his life as well as his victory over the holdup men. To Chum!

A great wave of love and gratitude surged up in Ferris. He had a sloppily idiotic yearning to throw his arms about the dog's furry neck and kiss him. But he steadied himself and chirped to the collie to come nearer. Slowly, with queer reluctance, Chum obeyed.

"Listen," mumbled Link incoherently, "I saved you from dying from a bust leg and hunger the night I fust met

41

you, Chummie. An' tonight you squared the bill by saving me from drownin'. But I'm still a whole lot in your debt, friend. I owe you for all the cash in my pocket an'—an' for a pint of the Stuff that Killed Father—an'—an' maybe for a beatin' that might of killed me. Chum, I guess God did a real day's work when He built you. I—I—Let it go at that. Only I ain't forgettin'. Nor yet I ain't li'ble to forget. Come on home. I'm a-gittin' the chatters!"

He had been stroking the oddly unresponsive dog's head as he spoke. Now, for the first time, Link realized that the night was cool, that his drenched clothes were like ice on him, and that the cold and the shock reaction were giving him a sharp congestive chill. Walking fast to restore circulation to his numbed body he made off for his distant farmhouse, Chum pattering along at his heels.

The rapid walk set him into a glow. But by the time he had reached home and had stripped off his wet clothes and swathed himself in a rough blanket, his racked nerves reasserted themselves. He craved a drink—a number of drinks—to restore his wonted poise. Lighting the kitchen lamp, he set the whisky bottle on the table and put a thick tumbler alongside it. Chum was lying at his master's feet. In front of Ferris was a pint of good cheer. The lamplight made the kitchen bright and cozy. Link felt a sense of utter well-being pervade him.

42

This was home—this was the real thing. Three successive and man-size drinks of whisky presently made it seem more and more the real thing. They made all things seem possible, and most things highly desirable. Link wanted to sing. And after two additional drinks he gratified this taste by lifting his voice in a hiccup-punctuated ditty addressed to one Jenny, whom the singer exhorted to wait till the clouds rolled by.

He was following this appeal by a rural lyric which recited in somewhat wearisome tonal monotony the adventures of a Little Black Bull that came Over the Mountain, when he observed that Chum was no longer lying at his feet. Indeed, the dog was in a far corner of the room, pressed close to the closed outer door, and with crest and ruff a-droop.

Puzzled by his pet's defection, Link imperiously commanded Chum to return to his former place. The collie, in most unwilling obedience, turned about and came slowly toward the drinker.

Every line of Chum's splendid body told of reluctance to approach his master. The deep-set, dark eyes were eloquent of a frightened disgust. He looked at Ferris as at some loathely stranger. The glad light of loyalty, which always had transfigured his visage when Link called to him, was woefully lacking. Drunk as he was Ferris could not help noticing the change. And he marveled at it.

"Whasser matter?" he demanded truculently. "What ails yer? C'm here, I'm tellin' you!"

He stretched out his hand in rough caress to the slowly approaching collie. Chum shrank back from the touch as a child from a dose of castor oil. There was no fear now in his aspect. Only disgust and a poignant unhappiness.

And, all suddenly, Link Ferris understood.

He himself did not know how the knowledge came to him. A canine psychologist might perhaps have told him that there is always an occult telepathy between the mind of a thoroughbred dog and its master, a power which gives them a glimpse into each other's processes of thought. But there was no such psychologist there to explain the thing. Nor did Link need it explained. It was enough for him that he knew.

He knew, as by revelation, that his adoring dog now shunned him because Link was drunk.

From the first, Chum's look of utter worship and his eagerly happy obedience had been a joy to Link. The subtly complete change in his worshiper's demeanor jarred sharply on the man's raw nerves. He felt vaguely unclean—shamed.

The contempt of such of his pious human neighbors as had passed him in the road during his sprees had affected Link not at all. Nor now could he understand the queer feeling of humiliation that swept over him at sight of the horrified repugnance in the eyes of this mere brute beast. It roused him to a gust of hot vexation.

"Shamed of me, are you?" he grunted fiercely. "A dirty four-legged critter's 'shamed of a he-man, hey? Well, we'll lick that out of you, dam' soon!"

Lurching to his feet, he snatched up a broom handle. He waved it menacingly over the dog. Chum gave back not an inch. Under the threat of a beating he stood his ground, his brave eyes steadfast, and, lurking in their mystic depths, that same glint of sorrowful wonder and disgust.

Up whirled the broomstick. But when it fell it did not smite athwart the shoulders of the sorrowing dog. Instead, it clattered harmlessly to the board floor. And to the floor also slumped Link Ferris, his nerve all gone, his heart soggy with sudden remorse.

To his knees thudded the man, close beside the collie. From Link's throat were bursting great strangled sobs which tortured his whole body and made his speech a tangled jumble that was not pretty to hear.

"Chum!" he wailed brokenly, clutching the dog's huge ruff in both shaky hands. "Chum, old friend! Gawd forgive me! You saved me from drowndin' an' from goin' broke, this night! You been the only friend that ever cared a hang if I was alive or dead! An'—an' I was goin' to lick you! I was goin' to lambaste you. Because I was a beastlier beast than YOU be. I was goin' to do it because you was so much better than me that you was made sick by my bein' a hawg. An' I was mad at you fer it. I'm—oh, I'm shameder than you are! Chum! Honest to Gawd, I am! Won't you make friends again? PLEASE, Chum!"

Now, of course, this was a most ridiculous and maudlin way to talk. Moreover, no man belongs on his knees beside a dog, even though the man be a sot and the dog a thoroughbred. In his calmer moments Link Ferris would have known this. A high-bred collie, too, has no use for sloppy emotion, but shuns its exhibition well-nigh as disgustedly as he shuns a drunkard.

Yet, for some illogical reason, Chum did not seek to withdraw his aristocratic self from the shivering clutch of the repentant souse. Instead, the expression of misery and repugnance fled as if by magic from his brooding eyes. Into them in its place leaped a light of keen solicitude. He pressed closer to the swayingly kneeling man, and with upthrust muzzle sought to kiss the blubbering face.

The whisky reek was as strong as ever. But something in Chum's soul was stronger. He seemed to know that the maudlin Unknown had vanished, and that his dear master was back again—his dear master who was in grievous trouble and who must be comforted.

Wherefore, the sickening liquor fumes no longer held him aloof from Link. Just as the icy lake had not deterred him from springing into the water after his drowning god, although, like most collies, Chum hated to swim.

Link, through his own nervous collapse, recognized the instant change in Chum's demeanor, and read it aright. It strengthened the old bond between himself and the dog. It somehow gave him a less scornful opinion of himself.

Presently he got to his feet, and with the collie at his side went back to the table, where stood the threeparts-empty flask. His face working, Link opened the window and poured what was left of the whisky out on the ground. There was nothing dramatic about his action. Rather it was tinged by very visible regret. Turning back to Chum, he said sheepishly:

"There it goes. An' I ain't sayin' I'm tickled at wastin' such good stuff. But—somehow I guess we've come to a showdown, Chum; you an' me. If I stick to booze, I'm li'ble to see you looking at me that queer way an' sidlin' away from me all the time; till maybe at last you'd get plumb sick of me for keeps, an' light out. An'—I'd rather have YOU than the booze, since I can't have both of you. Bein' only a dawg and never havin' tasted good red liquor, you can't know what a big bouquet I'm a-throwin' at you when I say that, neither. I—Oh, let's call it a day and go to sleep."

Next morning, in the course of nature, Link Ferris worked with a splitting headache. He carried it and a bad taste in his mouth, for the best part of the day.

But it was the last drink headache which marred his labor, all that long and happy summer. His work showed the results of the change. So did the meager hill farm. So did Link's system and his pocketbook.

As he was a real, live human and not a temperance tract hero, there were times when he girded bitterly at his self-enforced abstinence. Where were times, too—when he had a touch of malaria and again when the cutworms slaughtered two rows of his early tomatoes—when he yearned unspeakably for the solace of an evening at the Hampton tavern.

He had never been a natural drinker. Like many a better man he had drunk less for what he sought to get than for what he sought to forget. And with the departure of loneliness and the new interest in his home, he felt less the need for wet conviviality and for drugging his fits of melancholy.

The memory of Chum's grieving repulsion somehow stuck in Ferris's mind. And it served as a brake, more than once, to his tavernward impulses. Two or three times, also, when Link's babyish gusts of destructive bad temper boiled to the surface at some setback or annoyance, much the same wonderingly distressed look would creep into the collie's glance—a look as of one who is revolted by a dear friend's failure to play up to form. And to his own amused surprise, Ferris found himself trying to curb these outbursts.

To the average human, a dog is only a dog. To Ferris, this collie of his was the one intimate friend of his life. Unversed in the ways of dogs, he overestimated Chum, of course, and valued his society and his good opinion far more highly than the average man would have done. Thus, perhaps, his desire to stand well in the dog's esteem had in it more that was commendable than ludicrous. Or perhaps not.

If the strange association did much for Link, it did infinitely more for Chum. He had found a master who had no social interests in life beyond his dog, and who could and did devote all his scant leisure hours to association with that dog. Chum's sagacity and individuality blossomed under such intensive tutelage, as might that of a clever child who is the sole pupil of its teacher.

Link did not seek to make a trick dog of his pet. He taught Chum to shake hands, to lie down, to "speak" and one or two more simple accomplishments. It was by talking constantly to the collie, as to a fellow human, that he broadened the dog's intelligence. Chum grew to know and to interpret every inflection of Ferris's voice, every simple word he spoke and every gesture of his.

Apart from mere good fellowship the dog was proving of great use on the farm. Morning and night, Chum drove the sheep and the cattle to their respective pastures and then back to the barnyard at night. At the entrances to the pastures, now, Ferris had rigged up rude gates with "bar catch" fastenings—simple contrivances which closed by gravity and whose bars the dog was readily taught to shove upward with his nose.

It was thus a matter of only a few days to teach Chum to open or close the light gates. This trick has been taught to countless collies, of course, in Great Britain, and to many here. But Link did not know that. He felt like another Columbus or Edison, at his own genius in devising such a scheme; and he felt an inordinate pride in Chum for learning the simple exploit so quickly.

Of old, Link had fretted at the waste of time in taking out the sheep and cows and in going for them at night. This dual duty was now a thing of the past. Chum did the work for him, and reveled in the excitement of it. Chum also— from watching Link perform the task twice—had learned to drive the chickens out of the garden patches whenever any of them chanced to stray thither, and to scurry into the cornfield with harrowing barks of ejection when a flock of crows hovered hungrily above the newly-planted crops.

All of which was continual amusement to Chum, and a tremendous help to his owner.

Link, getting over his initial wonder at the dog's progress, began to take these accomplishments as a matter of course. Indeed, he was sometimes perplexed at the otherwise sagacious dog's limitations of brain.

For example, Chum loved the fire on the chilly evenings such as creep over the mountain region even in midsummer. He would watch Link replenish the blaze with fresh sticks whenever it sank low.

Yet, left to himself, he would let the fire go out, and he never knew enough to pick up a stick in his mouth and lay it on the embers. This lack of reasoning powers in his pet perplexed Ferris.

Link could not understand why the same wit which sent Chum half a mile, of his own accord, in search of one missing sheep out of the entire flock, should not tell him that a fire is kept alive by the putting of wood on it.

In search of some better authority on dog intelligence, Link paid his first visit to Hampton's little public library. There, shamefacedly, he asked the boy in charge for some books about dogs. The youth looked idly for a few minutes in a crossindex file. Then he brought forth a tome called "The Double Garden," written by someone who was evidently an Eyetalian or Polack or other foreigner, because he bore the grievously un-American name of "Maeterlinck".

"This is all I can find about dogs," explained the boy, passing the linen-jacketed little volume across the counter to Link. "First story in it is an essay on 'Our Friend, the Dog,' the index says. Want it?"

That evening, by his kitchen lamp, Ferris read laboriously the Belgian philosopher's dog essay. He read it aloud—as he had taken to thinking aloud—for Chum's benefit. And there were many parts of the immortal essay from which the man gleaned no more sense than did the collie.

It began with a promising account of a puppy named Pelleas. But midway it branched off into something else. Something Link could not make head nor tail of. Then, on second reading, bits of Maeterlinck's meaning, here and there, seeped into Ferris's bewilderedly groping intellect.

He learned, among other things, that Man is all alone on earth; that most animals don't know he is here, and that the rest of them have no use for him. That even flowers and crops will desert him and run again to wildness, if Man turns his back on them for a minute. So will his horse, his cow and his sheep. They graft on him for a living, and they hate or ignore him.

The dog alone, Link spelled out, has pierced the vast barrier between humans and other beasts, and has ranged himself, willingly and joyously, on the side of Man. For Man's sake the dog will not only starve and suffer and lay down his life, but will betray his fellow quadrupeds. Man is the dog's god. And the dog is the only living mortal that has the privilege of looking upon the face of his deity.

All of which was doubtless very interesting, and part of which thrilled Ferris, but none of which enlightened him as to a dog's uncanny wisdom in certain things and his blank stupidity in others. Next day Link returned the book to the library, no wiser than before, albeit with a higher appreciation of his own good luck in being the god of one splendid dog like Chum.

July had drowsed into August, and August was burning its sultry way toward September. Link's quarterly check from the Paterson Market arrived. And Ferris went as usual to the Hampton store to get it cashed. This tine he stood in less dire need of money's life-saving qualities than of yore. It had been a good summer for Link. The liquor out of his system and with a new interest in life, he had worked with a snap and vigor which had brought results in hard cash.

None the less, he was glad for this check. In another month the annual interest on his farm mortgage would fall due. And the meeting of that payment was always a problem. This year he would be less cruelly harassed by it than before.

Yet, all the more, he desired extra money. For a startlingly original ambition had awakened recently in his heart—namely, to pay off a little of the mortgage's principal along with the interest.

At first the idea had staggered him. But talking it over with Chum and studying his thumbed-soiled ledger, he had decided there was a bare chance he might be able to do it.

As he mounted the steps of the store, this evening in late August, he saw, tacked to the doorside clapboards, a truly gorgeous poster. By the light of the flickering lamp over the door, he discerned the vivid scarlet head of a dog in the upper corner of the yellow placard, and much display type below it.

It was the picture of the dog which checked Link in passing. It was a fancy head—the head of a stately and long muzzled dog with a ruff and with tulip ears. In short, just such a dog as Chum. Not knowing that Chum was a collie and that poster artists rejoice to depict collies, by reason of the latter's decorative qualities, Ferris was amazed by the coincidence.

After a long and critical survey of the picture, he was moved to run his eye over the flaring reading matter.

The poster announced, to all and sundry, that on Labor Day a mammoth dog show was to be held in the country club grounds at Craigswold—a show for the benefit of the Red Cross. Entries were to be one dollar for each class. "Thanks to generous contributions, the committee was enabled to offer prizes of unusual beauty and value, in addition to the customary ribbons."

Followed a list of cups and medals. Link scanned them with no great interest, But suddenly his roving gaze came to an astonished standstill. At the bottom of the poster, in forty-eight-point bold-face type, ran the following proclamation:

COL. CYRUS MARDEN

OF CRAIGSWOLD MANOR

OFFERS A CASH AWARD OF
ONE HUNDRED DOLLARS ($100) TO THE
BEST DOG OF ANY BREED EXHIBITED

One hundred dollars!

Link reread the glittering sentence until he could have said it backward. It would have been a patent lie had he heard it by word of mouth. But as it was in print, of course it was true.

One hundred dollars! And as a prize for the finest dog in the show. Not to BUY the dog, mind you. Just as a gift to the man who happened to own the best dog. It did not seem possible. Yet—

Link knew by hearsay and by observation the ways of the rich colony at Craigswold. He knew the Craigswolders spent money like mud, when it so pleased them—although more than one fellow huckster was at times sore put to it to collect from them a bill for fresh vegetables.

Yes, and he knew Col. Cyrus Marden by sight, too. He was a long-faced little man who used to go about dressed in funny knee pants and with a leather bag of misshapen clubs over his shoulder. Link had seen him again and again. He had seen the Colonel's enormous house at Craigswold Manor, too. He had no doubt Marden could afford this gift of a hundred dollars.

"TO THE BEST DOG OF ANY BREED!"

Ferris knew nothing about the various breeds of dogs. But he did know that Chum was by far the best and most beautiful and the wisest dog ever born. If Marden were offering a hundred dollar prize for the best dog, there was not another dog on earth fit to compete with Chum. That was a cinch.

As for the hundred dollars—why, it would be a godsend on the mortgage payment! Every cent of it could go toward the principal. That meant Ferris could devote the extra few dollars he had already saved for the principal to the buying of fertilizers and several sorely-needed utensils and to the shingling of the house.

Avid for more news of the offer, he entered the store and hunted up the postmaster, who also chanced to be the store's proprietor and the mayor of Hampton and the local peace justice. Of this Pooh-Bah the inquiring Ferris sought for details.

"Some of the Red Cross ladies from up Craigswold way were here this morning, to have me nail that sign on the store," reported the postmaster. "They're making a tour of all the towns hereabouts. They asked me to try to int'rest folks at Hampton in their show, too, and get them to make entries. They left me a bunch of blanks. Want one?"

"Yep," said Link. "I guess I'll take one if it don't cost nothin', please."

He studied the proffered entry blank with totally uncomprehending gaze. The postmaster came to his relief.

"Let me show you," he suggested, taking pity on his customer's wrinkled brow and squinting helplessness. "I've had some experience in this folderol. I took my Airedale over to the Ridgewood show last spring and got a third with him. I'm going to take him up to Craigswold on Labor Day, too. What kind of dog is yours?"

"The dandiest dawg that ever stood on four legs," answered Link, afire with the zeal of ownership. "Why, that dawg of mine c'n—"

"What breed is he?" asked the postmaster, not interested in the dawning rhapsody.

"Oh—breed?" repeated Link. "Why, I don't rightly know. Some kind of a bird dawg, I guess. Yes. A bird dawg. But he's sure the grandest—"

"Is he the dog you had down here, one day last month?" asked the postmaster, with a gleam of recollection.

"Yep. That's him," assented Link. "Only dawg I've got. Only dawg I ever had. Only dawg I ever want to have. He's—"

But the postmaster was not attending. His time was limited. So, taking out a fountain pen, he had begun to scribble on the blank. Filling in Link's name and address, he wrote, in the "breed and sex" spaces, the words, "Scotch collie, sable-and-white, male."

"Name?" he queried, breaking in on Ferris's rambling eulogy.

"Huh?" asked the surprised Link, adding: "Oh, his name, hey? I call him 'Chum.' You see, that dawg's more like a chum to me than—"

"No use asking about his pedigree, I suppose," resumed the postmaster, "I mean who his parents were and—"

"Nope," said Link. "I—I found him. His leg was—"

"Pedigree unknown," wrote the postmaster; then, "What classes are you entering him for?"

"Classes?" repeated Link dully. "Why, I just want to put him into that contest for 'best dawg,' you see. He—"

"Hold on!" interposed the postmaster impatiently. "You don't catch the idea. In each breed there are a certain number of classes: 'Puppy,' 'Novice,' 'Limit,' 'Open,' and so on. The dogs that get a blue ribbon—that's first prize—in these classes all have to appear in what is called the 'Winners Class.' Then the dog that gets 'Winner's'—the dog that gets first prize in this 'Winners' Class'—competes for best dog of his breed in the show. After that—as a 'special'—the best in all the different breeds are brought into the ring. And the dog that wins in that final class is adjudged the 'best in the show.' He's the dog in this particular show that will get Colonel Marden's hundred-dollar cash prize. See what I mean?"

"Ye-es," replied Link, after digesting carefully what he had heard. "I guess so. But—"

"Since you've never shown your dog before," went on the postmaster, beginning to warm with professional interest, "you can enter him in the 'Novice Class.' That's generally the easiest. If he loses in that, no harm's done. If he wins he has a chance later in the 'Winners' Class.' I'm mailing my entry to-night to the committee. If you like, I'll send yours along with it. Give me a dollar."

While Link extracted a greasy dollar bill from his pocket, the postmaster filled in the class space with the word "Novice."

"Thanks for helpin' me out," said Ferris, grateful for the lift.

"That's all right," returned the postmaster, pocketing the bill and folding the blank, as he prepared to end the interview by moving away. "Be sure to have your dog at the gate leading into the Craigswold Country Club grounds promptly at ten o'clock on Labor Day. If you don't get a card and a tag sent to you, before then, tell your name to the clerk at the table there, and he'll give you a number. Tie your dog to the stall with that number on it, and be sure to have him ready to go into the ring when his number is called. That's all."

"Thanks!" said Link, again. "An' now I guess I'll go back home an' commence brightenin' Chum up, a wee peckle, on his tricks. Maybe I'll have time to learn him some new ones, too. I want him to make a hit with them judges, an' everything."

"Tricks?" scoffed the postmaster, pausing as he started to walk away. "Dogs don't need tricks in the show ring. All you have to do is to lead your dog into the ring, and parade him round with the rest of them till the judge tells you to stop. Then he'll make them stand on the show platform while he examines them. The dog's only 'tricks' are to stand and walk at his best, and to look alert, so the judge can see the shape of his ears and get his expression. Teach your dog to walk around with you, on the leash, without hanging back, and to prick up his ears and stand at attention when you tell him to. That's all he needs to do. The judge will do the rest. Have him clean and well brushed, of course."

"I—I sure feel bitter sorry for there other dawgs at the show!" mumbled Link. "A hundred dollars! Of all the dawgs that ever happened, Chummie is that one! Why, there ain't a thing he can't do, from herdin' sheep to winnin' a wad of soft money! An'—an' he's all MINE."

CHAPTER III.

The Ordeal

By dawn on Labor Day Link Ferris was astir. A series of discomfiting baths and repeated currying with the dandy brush had made Chum's grand coat stand out in shimmering fluffiness. A course of carefully-conducted circular promenades on the end of a chain had taught the dog to walk gaily and unrestrainedly in leash. And any of several cryptic words, relating to hypothetical rats, and so forth, were quite enough to send up his ears.

It was sheer excitement that brought Link broad awake before sunrise on that day of days. Ferris was infected with the most virulent form of that weird malady known as "dog-showitis." At first he had been tempted solely by the hope of winning the hundred-dollar prize. But latterly the urge of victory had gotten into his blood. And he yearned, too, to let the world see what a marvelous dog was his.

He hurried through the morning chores, then dressed himself in his shabby best and hitched his horse to the antiquated Concord buggy—a vehicle he had been washing for the state occasion almost as vehemently as he had scrubbed Chum.

After a gobbled breakfast, Ferris mounted to the seat of the aged buggy, signaled Chum to leap to the battered

61

cushion at his side and set off for Craigswold. Long before ten o'clock his horse was safely stabled at the Craigswold livery, and Ferris was leading Chum proudly through the wicket gate leading into the country-club grounds.

All happened as the postmaster had foretold. The clerk at the wicket asked him his name, fumbled through a ledger and a pile of envelopes and presently handed Ferris a numbered tag.

"Sixty-five," read the clerk for Link's benefit. "That's down at the extreme right. Almost the last bench to the right."

Into the hallowed precinct Link piloted the much-interested Chum. There he paused for a dazzled instant. The putting green and the fore-lawn in front of the field-stone clubhouse had been covered with a mass of wooden alleyways, each lined with a double row of stalls about two feet from the ground, carpeted with straw and having individual zinc water troughs in front of them. In nearly every one of these "benches" was tied a dog.

There were more dogs than Link Ferris had seen before in all his quasi-dogless life. And all of them seemed to be barking or yelping. The din was egregious. Along the alleyways, men and women in sport clothes were drifting, in survey of the chained exhibits. In a central space among the lines of benches was a large square enclosure, roped off except for one aperture. In the middle of this space, which

Link rightly guessed to be the judging ring, stood a very low wooden platform. At one side of the ring were a chair and a table, where sat a steward in a Palm Beach suit, fussily turning over the leaves of a ledger and assorting a heap of high-packed and vari-colored ribbons.

Link, mindful of instructions, bore to the right in search of a stall labeled "65." As he went, he noted that the dogs were benched in such a way that each breed had a section to itself. Thus, while he was still some distance away from his designated bench, he saw that he was coming into a section of dogs which, in general aspect, resembled Chum. Above this aggregation, as over others, hung a lettered sign. And this especial sign read "Collie Section."

So Chum was a "collie"—whatever that might be. Link took it to be a fancy term for "bird dog." He had seen the word before somewhere. And he remembered now that it had been in the advertisement that offered seventy-five dollars for the return of a lost "sable-and-white collie." Yes, and Dominie Jansen had said, "sable" meant "black." Link felt a glow of relief that the advertisement had not said "a brown-and-white collie."

Chum was viewing his new surroundings with much attention, looking up now and then into his master's face as they moved along the rackety line—as though to gain reassurance that all was well.

To a high-strung and sensitive dog a show is a terrific ordeal. But Chum, like the aristocrat he was, bore its preliminaries with debonair calm.

Arriving at Bench 65 in the collie section, Link enthroned his dog there, fastening the chain's free end to a ring in the stall's corner. Then, after seeing that the water pan was where Chum could reach it in case he were thirsty and that the straw made a comfortable couch for him, Ferris once more patted the worried dog and told him everything was all right. After which Link proceeded to take a survey of the neighboring collies, the sixteen dogs which were to be Chum's competitors.

His first appraising glance of the double row of collies caused the furrow between his eyes to vanish and brought a grin of complacent satisfaction to his thin lips. For he did not see a single entrant that, in his eyes, seemed to have a ghost of a chance against his idolized pet—not a dog as handsome or with half the look of intelligence or with the proudly gay bearing of Chum.

Of the sixteen other collies the majority were sables of divers shades. There were three tricolors and two mist-hued merles. Over nearly all the section's occupants a swarm of owners and handlers were just now busy with brush and cloth. For word had come that collies were to be the second breed judged that day. The first breed was to be the Great Danes. As there were but three Danes in the show, their judging would be brief. And it behooved the collies' attendants to have their entries ready.

Link, following the example of those around him, took from his pocket the molting dandy brush and set to work once more on Chum's coat. He observed that the rest were brushing their dogs' fur against the grain, to make it fluff up. And he reversed his own former process in imitation of them. He had supposed until now that a collie's hair, like a man's, ought to be slicked down smooth for state occasions. And it troubled him to find that Chum's coat rebelled against such treatment. Now, under the reverse process, it stood out in wavy freedom.

At the adjoining stall to the left a decidedly pretty girl was watching a groom put the finishing touches to the toilet of her tricolor collie. Link heard her exclaim in protest as the groom removed from the dog's collar a huge cerise bow she had just affixed there.

"Sorry, Miss," Ferris heard the groom explain, "but it's agin rules for a dog to go in the ring with a ribbon on. If the judge thinks he's good enough for a ribbon he'll award him one. But—"

"Oh, he simply can't help awarding one to Morven, here!" broke in the girl. "CAN he, Stokes?"

"Hard to say, Miss," answered the groom imperturbably, as he wrought with brush and cloth. "Judges has their own ideas. We'll have to hope for the best for him and not be too sick if he gets gated."

"Gated?" echoed the girl—an evident newcomer to the realm of showdom.

"Yes, Miss," expounded the groom. "'Gated' means 'shown the gate.' Some judges thins out a class that way, by sending the poorest dogs out of the ring first. Then again, some judges—"

"Oh, I'm glad I wore this dress!" sighed the girl. "It goes so well with Morven's color. Perhaps the judge—"

"Excuse me, Miss," put in the groom, trying not to laugh, "but the collie judge to-day is Fred Leightonhe bred the great Howgill Rival, you know—and when Leighton is in the ring, he hasn't got eyes for anything but the dogs themselves. Begging your pardon, he wouldn't notice if you was to wear a horse blanket. At that, Leighton's the squarest and the best—"

"Look!" whispered the girl, whose attention had wandered and whose roving gaze had settled on Chum. "Look at that dog in the next bench. Isn't he magnificent?"

Link swelled with pride at the lowspoken praise. And turning away to hide his satisfaction, he saw that quite a sizable knot of spectators had gathered in front of Chum's bench. They were inspecting the collie with manifest approval. Chum, embarrassed by the unaccustomed notice, had moved as far as possible from his admirers, and was nuzzling his head into Ferris's hand for refuge.

"Puppy Class, Male Scotch Collies!" droned a ring attendant, appearing for a moment at the far end of the section. "Numbers 60, 61, 62."

Three youngsters, ranging in age from seven to eleven months, were coaxed down from their straw couches by three excited owners and were convoyed fussily toward the ring.

"Novice Class next, Miss," Link heard the groom saying to the girl at the adjoining bench. "Got his ring leash ready?"

"Ring leash!" This was a new one to Ferris. His eyes followed the trio of puppies shuffling ringward. He saw that all three were on leather leashes and that their chains had been left in the stalls. Presumably there was a law against chains in the ring. And Link had no leash.

For an instant he was in a quandary. Then his brow cleared. True, he had no leash. Yet, if chains, like bows of ribbon, were barred from the ring, he could maneuver Chum every bit as well with his voice as with any leash. So that problem was solved.

A minute later, the three pups reappeared at the end of the section. And behind them came the attendant, intoning:

"Novice Class, Male Scotch Collies! Numbers 64, 65, 66, 67."

There was an absurd throbbing in Link Ferris's meridian. His calloused hands shook as he unchained Chum and motioned him to leap from the bench to the ground.

Chum obeyed, but with evident uneasiness. His odd surroundings were getting on the collie's nerves. Link bent over him, under pretense of giving him a farewell rub with the brush.

"It's all right, Chummie!" he crooned soothingly. "It's all RIGHT! I'm here. An' nobody's goin' to bother you none. You're a-helpin' me win that hundred. An' you're lettin' these gold-shirt folks see what a clam' gorgeous dawg you be! Come along, ol' friend!"

Under the comfort of his god's voice, Chum's nervousness fled. Safe in his sublime trust that his master would let no harm befall him, the collie trotted toward the ring at Ferris's heels.

Three other novice dogs were already in the ring when Link arrived at the narrow opening. The steward was sitting at the table as before. At the corner of the ring, alongside the platform, stood a man in tweeds, unlighted pipe in mouth, half-shut shrewd eyes studying the dogs as they filed in through the gap in the ropes. The inscrutable eyes flickered ever so little at sight of Chum, but at once resumed their former disinterested gaze.

"Walk close!" whispered Link as the parade started.

Chum, hearing a command he had long since learned, ranged himself at Ferris's side and paced majestically in the procession of four. Two of the other novice dogs were straining at their leashes; the third was hanging back and pawing frantically to break away. Chum, unleashed, guided only by the voice, drew every eye to him by his rare beauty and his lofty self-possession.

But he was not allowed to finish the parade. Stepping up to Ferris, Judge Leighton tapped him on the arm.

"Take your dog over to that corner," he ordered, "and keep him there."

Link fought back a yearning to punch the judge, and surlily he obeyed the mandate. Into his memory jumped the things the groom had said about a dog being "gated." If that judge thought for one second that any of those mutts could hold a candle to Chum—. Again he yearned to enforce with his two willing fists his opinion of the judge.

But, as he well knew, to start a fight in this plutocratic assemblage would mean a jail term. And in such case, what would befall the deserted Chum? For the dog's sake he restrained himself, and he began to edge surreptitiously toward the ring exit, with a view to sliding out unperceived with his splendid, underrated dog.

But Ferris did not reach the gate unchecked.

Judge Leighton had ended the parade and had stood the three dogs, one by one and then two at a time, on the platform while he studied them. Then he had crossed to the table and picked up the judging book and four ribbons— one blue, one red, one yellow and one white. Three of these ribbons he handed to the three contestants' handlers.

Then he stepped across the ring to where Ferris was edging his way toward the exit; and handed Link the remaining ribbon. It was dark blue, with gilt lettering.

Leighton did not so much as subject Chum to the handling and close inspection he had lavished on the three others. One expert glance had told the judge that the dark-sable collie, led by this loutish countryman, was better fitted to clean up prizes at Madison Square Garden than to appear in a society dog show in the North Jersey hinterland.

Leighton had viewed Chum, as a bored musician, listening to the piano-antics of defective children, might have regarded the playing of a disguised Paderewski. Wherefore, he had waved the dog to one side while he judged the lesser entrants, and then had given him the merited first-prize ribbon.

Link, in a daze of bliss, stalked back to the bench; with Chum capering along at his side. The queer sixth sense of a collie told Chum his god was deliriously happy, and that Chum himself had somehow had a share in making him so. Hence the dog's former gloomy pacing changed to a series of ecstatic little dance steps, and he kept thrusting his cold muzzle into the cup of Ferris's palm.

Again Bench 65 was surrounded by an admiring clump of spectators. Chum and Link vied each other in their icy aloofness toward these admirers. But with a difference.

Chum was unaffectedly bothered by so much unwelcome attention from strangers. Ferris, on the other hand, reveled in the knowledge that his beloved pet was the center of more adulation than was any other dog in all the section.

Class after class went to be judged. Link was sorry he had not spent more money and entered Chum in every class. The initial victory had gone to his head. He had not known he could be so serenely happy. After a while, he started up at the attendant's droning announcement of,

"Winners' Class, Male Scotch Collies! Numbers 62, 65, 68,70, 73!"

Again Link and Chum set out for the ring. Link's glee had merged into an all-consuming nervousness, comparable only to a maiden hunter's "buck ague." Chum, once more sensing Ferris's state of mind, lost his own glad buoyancy and paced solemnly alongside, peering worriedly up into Link's face at every few steps.

All five entrants filed into the ring and began their parade. Leighton, in view of the importance of this crowning event, did not single out any one dog, as before, to stand to one side; nor did he gate any. He gave owners and spectators their full due, by a thorough inspection of all five contestants. But as a result of his examination, he ended the suspense by handing Link Ferris a purple rosette, whereon was blazoned in gilt the legend, "Winners."

A salvo of handclaps greeted the eminently just decision. And Chum left the ring, to find a score of gratulatory hands stretched forth to pat him. Quite a little crowd escorted him back to his bench.

A dozen people picked acquaintance with Link. They asked him all sorts of questions as to his dog. Link made monosyllabic and noncommittal replies to all of these—even when the great Col. Cyrus Marden himself deigned to come over to the collie section and stare at Chum, accompanying his scrutiny with a volley or patronizing inquiries.

From the bystanders Link learned something of real interest—namely, that one of the "specials" was a big silver cup, to be awarded to "best collie of either sex"; and that after the females should have been, judged, the winning female and Chum must appear in the ring together to compete for this trophy.

Sure enough, in less than thirty minutes Chum was summoned to the ring. There, awaiting him, was a dainty and temperamental merle, of the Tazewell strain. Exquisite and high-bred as was this female competitor, Judge Leighton wasted little time on the examination before giving Ferris a tricolored ribbon, whose possession entitled him to one of the shimmering silver mugs in the near-by trophy case.

After receiving full assurance that the big cup should be his at the close of the show, Link returned to Chum's bench in ecstasy and sat down beside his tired dog, with one arm thrown lovingly round the collie's ruff. Chum nestled against his triumphant master, as Link fondled his bunch of ribbons and went over, mentally, every move of his triumphal morning.

The milling and changing groups of spectators in front of Bench 65 did not dwindle. Indeed, as the morning went on, they increased. People kept coming back to the bench and bringing others with them. Some of these people whispered together. Some merely stared and went away. Some asked Ferris carefully worded questions, to which the shyly happy mountaineer replied with sheepish grunts.

The long period of judging came at last to an end. And the "Best Dog in Show" special was called.

Into the ring Ferris escorted Chum, amid a multitude of fellow winners, representing one male or female of every breed exhibited. Leighton and another judge stood in the ring's center, and around them billowed the heterogeneous array. The two went at their Gargantuan task with an expert swiftness. Mercilessly, dog after dog was weeded out and gated. At last, Chum and two others were all remaining of the many which had thronged the ring. The spectators were banked, five deep and breathless, round the ropes.

The two judges went into brief executive session in one corner. Then Leighton crossed to Link, for the fourth time that day, and gave him the gaudy rosette which proclaimed Chum "best dog in the show." A roar of applause went up. Link felt dizzy—and numb. Then, with a gasp of rapture, he stooped and gathered the bored Chum in his long arms, in a bearlike, ecstatic hug.

"We done it, Chummie!" he chortled. "WE DONE IT!"

Still in a daze, he followed the steward to the trophy case, where he received not only the shining silver cup, but a "sovereign purse," wherein were ensconced ten ten-dollar gold pieces.

It was all a dream—a wonder dream from which presently he must awaken. Link was certain of that. But while the golden dream lasted, he knew the nameless joys of paradise.

Chum close at his side, he made his way through the congratulating crowd toward the outer gate of the country club grounds. He had almost reached the wicket when someone touched him, with unnecessary firmness, on the shoulder.

Not relishing the familiarity, Link turned a scowling visage on the interrupter of his triumphal homeward progress. At his elbow stood a stockily-built man, dressed with severe plainness.

"You're Lincoln Ferris?" queried the stranger, more as if stating aggressively a fact than making an inquiry.

"Yep," said Link, cross at this annoying break-in upon his trance of happiness. "What d'j' want?" he added.

"Please step back to the clubhouse a minute with me," returned the stranger, civilly enough, but with the same bossy firmness in his tone that had jarred Ferris in his touch. "One or two people want to speak to you. Bring along your dog."

Link glowered. He fancied he knew what was in store. Some of the ultra select had gathered in the holy interior of the clubhouse and wanted a private view of Chum, unsullied by the noisy presence of the crowd outside. They would talk patronizingly to Link, and perhaps even try to coax him into selling Chum. The thought decided Ferris.

"I'm goin' home!" he said roughly.

"You're coming with me," contradicted the man in that same quiet voice, but slipping his muscular arm into Link's.

With his other hand he shifted the lapel of his coat, displaying a police badge on its reverse. Still avoiding any outward appearance of force, he turned about, with his arm locked in Ferris's and started toward the clubhouse.

"Here!" expostulated poor Link, with a true mountaineer's horror of the police. "What's all this? I ain't broke no law! I—"

An ugly growl from Chum punctuated his scared plea. Noting the terror in his master's tone and the grip of the stranger on Link's arm, Chum had spun round to face the two.

The collie's eyes were fixed grimly upon the plainclothes man's temptingly thick throat. One corner of Chum's upper lip was curled back, displaying a businesslike if snowy fang. His head was lowered. Deep in his furry throat a succession of legato growls were born.

The plain-clothes man knew much about dogs. He knew, for example, that when a dog holds his head high and barks there is no special danger to be feared from him. But he also knew that when a dog lowers his head and growls, showing his eyetooth, he means business.

And the man shrank from the menace. One hand crept back instinctively toward his hip pocket.

Link saw the purely involuntary gesture, and he shook in his boots. It was thus a Hampton constable had once reached back when a stray cur snapped at him. And that constable had completed the movement by drawing a pistol and shooting the cur. Perhaps this non-uniformed stranger meant to do the same thing.

"Hold on!" begged Link, intervening between the man and the dog. "I'll go along with you peaceful. Quit, Chum! It's all right!"

The dog still looked undecided. He did not like this new note in his god's voice. But he obeyed the injunction, and fell into step at Link's side as usual. Ferris suffered himself to be piloted, unresisting, through the tattered remnant of the crowd and up the clubhouse steps.

There his conductor led him through the sacred portals and down a wide hallway to the door of a committee room. Throwing open the door, he ushered in his captive and the dog, entering behind them and reclosing the heavy door.

In the room, round a table, sat several persons—all men except one. The exception was the girl whose collie had had the bench next to Chum's. At the table head, looking very magisterial indeed, sat Colonel Marden. Beside him lounged a larger and older man in a plaid sport suit.

Link's escort ranged his prisoners at the foot of the table; Chum standing tight against Ferris's knee, as if to guard him from possible harm. Link stood glowering in sullen perplexity at the Colonel. Marden cleared his voice pompously, then spoke.

"Ferris," he began with much impressiveness, "I am a magistrate of this county—as you perhaps know. You may consider yourself before the Bar of Justice, and reply to my questions accordingly."

Awed by this thundered preamble, Ferris made shift to mutter:

"I ain't broke no laws. What d'j' want of me, anyhow?"

"First of all," proceeded Marden, "where did you get that dog?"

"Chum here?" said Ferris. "Why, I come acrost him, early last spring, on the patch of state road, jes' outside of Hampton. He was a-layin' in a ditch, with his leg bust. Throwed off'n a auto, I figgered it. I took him home an'—"

He paused, as the sport-suited man next to Marden nodded excitedly to the girl and then whispered to the Colonel.

"You took him home?" pursued Marden. "Couldn't you see he was a valuable dog?"

"I c'd see he was a sufferin' an' dyin' dawg," retorted Link. "I c'd see he was a goner, 'less I took him home an' 'tended him. If you're aimin' at findin' out why I went on keepin' him after that, I done so because no one claimed him. I put up notices 'bout him. I put one up at the post-office here, too. I—"

"He did!" interrupted the girl. "That's true! I saw it. Only—the notice said it was a bird dog. That's why we didn't follow it up. He—"

"Miss Gault," suggested Marden in lofty reproof, "suppose you leave the interrogatory to me, if you please? Yes, I recollect that notice. My attention was called to it at the time. But," again addressing Link, "why did you call

'Glenmuir Cavalier' a 'BIRD dog'? Was it to throw us off the track or—"

"Don't know no What's-His-Name Cav'lier!" snapped Ferris. "This dawg's name is Chum. Like you c'n see in my entry blank, what's layin' on the table in front of you. I adv'tised Chum as a bird dawg because I s'posed he WAS a bird dawg. I ain't a sharp on dawgs. He's the fust one ever I had. If he ain't a bird dawg, 'tain't my fault. He looks more like one than like 'tother breeds I'd seen. So I called him one."

"There is no need to raise your voice at me!" rebuked the colonel. "I am disposed to accept your explanation. But if you read the local papers you must have seen—"

"I did read 'em," said Ferris. "I read 'em steady for a month or more, to see was there was adv'tisement fer a lost dawg. Nary an adv'tisement did I see excep' one fer a 'sable' collie. 'Sable' means 'black.' I know, because our dominie told me so. I asked him, when I see that piece in the paper. Chum ain't black, nor nowheres near black. So I knowed it couldn't be him. What d'j' want of me, anyhow?" he demanded once more.

"Again, I am disposed to credit your explanation," boomed the colonel, frowning down a ripple of giggles that had its rise in Miss Gault. "And I am disposed to acquit you of consciously dishonest intent. I am glad to do so. Here is the situation: Early last spring, Mr. Gault," indicating the sport-suit wearer at his left, "bought from the famous Glenmuir Collie Kennels, on the Hudson, an unusually fine young collie—a dog for which connoisseurs predicted a great future in the show ring. He purchased it as a gift for his daughter, Miss Marion Gault."

He inclined his head slightly toward the girl; then proceeded:

"As Mr. Glenmuir was disbanding his kennel, Mr. Gault was able to secure the dog—Glenmuir Cavalier. He started for Craigswold, with the dog on the rear seat of the car. At first he kept a hand on the dog's collar, but as the collie made no attempt to escape, he soon turned around—he was in the front seat—and paid no more attention to him. Just outside of Suffern, he looked back—to find Cavalier had disappeared. He advertised, and made all possible efforts to locate the dog. But he could get no clew to him, until to-day. Seeing this dog of yours in the show ring, he recognized him at once."

The pompously booming voice, with its stilted diction, ceased. All eyes were upon Link Ferris. The mountaineer, stung to life by the silence and the multiple gaze, came out of his trance of shock.

"Then—then," he stuttered, forcing the words from a throat sanded by sudden dread, "then Chum rightly b'longs to this man?"

"Quite so!" assented Marden, in some relief. "I am glad you grasp the point so readily. Mr. Gault has talked the matter over with me, and he is taking a remarkably broad and generous view of the case if I may say so. He is not only willing that you should keep the cup and the cash prize which you have won to-day, but he is also ready to pay to you the seventy-five dollar reward he offered for the return of Glenmuir Cavalier. I repeat, this strikes me as most gener—"

"NO!" yelled Link, a spasm of foreseen loneliness sweeping over him. "NO!! He can't have him! Nobody can! Why Chum's my dawg! I've learned him to fetch cows an' shake hands an'—an' everything! An' he drug me out'n the lake, when I was a-drownin'! An' he done a heap more'n that fer me! He's drug me up to my feet, out'n wuthlessness, too; an' he's learned me that livin' is wuth while! He's my— my—he's my dawg!" he finished lamely, his scared eyes sweeping the circle of faces in panic appeal.

"That will do, Ferris!" coldly exhorted the colonel. "We wish no scenes here. You will take this seventyfive dollar check which Mr. Gault has so kindly made out for you, and you will go."

"Leavin' Chum behind?" babbled Ferris, aghast. "Not leavin' Chum behind? PLEASE not!"

He pulled himself together with an effort that drove his nails bitingly into his palms and left his face gray. He saw the uselessness of pleading with these people of polished iron, who could not understand his fearful loss. For the sake of Chum—for the sake of the self-respecting man he himself had become—he would not let himself go to pieces. Forcing his shaken voice to a dry steadiness, he addressed the uneasily squirming Gault.

"What d'j' you pay for Chum when you bought him off'n that Hudson River feller—that Glenmuir chap?" he demanded.

"Why, as a matter of fact," responded Gault, "as Colonel Marden has told you, I couldn't have hoped to get such a promising collie at any price it—"

"What d'j' you pay for him?" insisted Link, his voice harsh and unconsciously domineering as a vague new hope dawned on his troubled mind.

"I paid six hundred dollars," answered Gault shortly, in annoyance at the boor's manner.

"Good!" approved Link, "That gives us suthin' to go on. I'll pay you six hundred dollars fer him back. This hundred dollars in gold an' this yer silver cup an' seven dollars more I got with me—to bind the bargain. An' a second mortgage on my farm fer the rest. Fer as much of the rest," he amended, "as I ain't got ready cash for."

In his stark earnestness, Link's rough voice sounded more hectoring and unpleasant than before. Gault, unused to such talk from the alleged "peasantry," resolved to cut short the haggling.

"Sell for six hundred a dog that's cleaned up 'best in the show?'" he rasped. "No, thank you. Leighton says Cavalier will go far. One man, ten minutes ago, offered me a thousand for him."

"A thousan'?" repeated Ferris, scared at the magnitude of the sum—then, rallying, he asked:

"What WILL you let me have him fer, then? Set a price, can't you?"

"The dog is not for sale," curtly replied Gault, busying himself with the lighting of a cigarette.

"Take Mr. Gault's check and go," commanded Marden, thrusting the slip of paper at Link. "I think there is nothing more to say. I have an appointment at—"

He hesitated. Regardless of the others' presence, Ferris dropped to one knee beside the uncomprehending dog. With his arm about Chum's neck, he bent close to the collie's ear and whispered:

"Good-by, Chummie! It's good-by, fer keeps, too. Don't you get to thinkin' I've gone an' deserted you, nor got tired of you, nor nothnn', Chum. Because I'd a dam' sight ruther leave one of my two legs here than to leave you. I—I guess only Gawd rightly knows all you done fer me, Chum. But I ain't a-goin' to ferget none of it. Lord, but it's goin' to be pretty turrible, to home, without you!" He got to his feet, winking back a mist from his red eyes, and turning blindly toward the door.

"Here!" boomed Marden after him. "You've forgotten your check."

"I don't aim to take no measly money fer givin' up the only friend I got!" snarled Link over his shoulder. "Keep it—fer a tip!"

It was a good exit line. But it was spoiled. Because, as Ferris reached the door and groped for its knob, Chum was beside him—glad to get out of this uncongenial assembly and to be alone with the master who seemed so unhappy and so direly in need of consolation. Link stiffened to his full height. With one hand lovingly laid on the collie's silken head, he mumbled:

"No, Chum, you can't come along. Back, boy! Stay HERE!"

Lowering at Gault, he added:

"He ain't never been hit, nor yet swore at. An' he don't need to be. Treat him nice, like he's used to bein' treated. An' don't get sore on him if he mopes fer me, jes' at fust. Because he's sure to. Dogs ain't like folks. They got hearts. Folks has only got souls. I guess dogs has the best of it, at that."

Ferris swung open the door and stumbled out, not trusting himself for a backward glance at the wistfully grieved dog he had left behind.

Lurchingly he made off, across the lawn and out through the wicket. He was numb and sick. He moved mechanically and with no conscious power of thought or of locomotion.

Out in the highroad, a homing instinct guided his leaden feet in the direction of Hampton. And he plodded dazedly the interminable four miles that separated him from his desolate farm.

As he turned in at his own gate, he was aware of a poignant dread that pierced his numbness. And he knew it for a dread of entering the house and of finding no one to welcome him. Setting his teeth he went forward, unlocked the door and stamped into the silent kitchen.

Upon the table he dumped the paper-swathed cup he had been carrying unnoticed under his arm. Beside it he threw the little purse full of gold pieces and the wad of prize ribbons. Stepping back, his foot struck something. He looked down and saw it was a gay-colored rubber ball he had bought, months ago, for Chum—the dog's favorite plaything.

His face twisting, Link snatched up the ball and went out onto the steps to throw it far out of sight; that it might no more remind him of the pet who had so often coaxed him to toss it for retrieval.

Ferris hurled the ball far out into the garden. As the missile left his hand an exultant bark re-echoed through the silence of the sunset. Chum, who had been trotting demurely up the walk, sprang gleefully in pursuit of the ball, and presently came galloping back to the dazedly incredulous Link, with the many-colored sphere of rubber between his jaws.

Chum had had no trouble at all in catching his master's trail and following it home. He would have overtaken the slow-slouching Ferris, had he been able to slip out of the clubhouse sooner. And now it pleased him to be welcomed by this evident invitation to a game of ball.

Link gave a gulping cry and buried both hands in the collie's ruff, staring down at the dancing dog in an agony of rapture. Then, all at once, his muscles tensed, and his newly flushed face went green-white again.

"I—I guess we got to play it square, Chum!" he muttered aloud, with something like a groan. "I was blattin' to 'em, up there, how you'd made a white man of me. An' a reg'lar white man don't keep what ain't his own prop'ty. Come along, Chummie!"

His jaw very tense, his back painfully stiff, Link strode heavily down the lane and out into the highroad. Chum, always eager for a walk with his god, frisked about him in delight.

He had traversed the bulk of the distance to Craigswold, the dog beside him, when he remembered that he had left his horse and buggy at the livery stable there in the morning.

Well, that would save his aching feet a four-mile walk home. In the meantime—

He and Chum stepped to the roadside to avoid a fast-traveling little motor car which was bearing down on them from the direction of Craigswold.

The car did not pass them. Instead, it came to a gear-racking halt close beside Ferris. Link, glancing up in dull lack of interest, beheld Gault and the latter's daughter staring down at him.

"Chum came home," said Ferris, scowling at them. "He trailed me. Don't lick him fer it! He's only a dog, an' he didn't know no better. I was bringin' him back to you."

The girl looked sharply at her father. Gault fidgeted uneasily, as he had done once or twice that afternoon in the clubhouse. And he avoided his daughter's gaze. So she turned her level eyes on Link.

"Mr. Ferris," she said very quietly, "do you mean to say, when this dog came back to you, you were actually going to return him to us, instead of hiding him somewhere till the search was over?"

"I'm here, ain't I?" countered Ferris defiantly.

"But why?" she insisted. "WHY?"

"Because I'm a fool, I s'pose," he growled. "I guess Chum wouldn't care much 'bout livin' with a thief. Take him up there with you on the seat. Don't let him fall out. An'"—his voice scaling a half octave in its pain—"keep him

87

to home after this. I ain't no measly angel. I can't swear I'd have the grit to fetch him back another time."

He stopped, to note a curious phenomenon. There were actually tears in the girl's big grave eyes. Link wondered why. Then she said:

"Cavalier isn't my father's dog. He is mine. My father gave him to me when he bought him, last spring. Colonel Marden seemed to have forgotten that to-day. And I didn't want to start a squabble by reminding him of it. After all, it's my father's affair, and mine. Nobody else's. My father got me another collie last spring to take Cavalier's place. A collie I'm ever so fond of. So I don't need Cavalier. I don't want him. I tried to find you to tell you so. But you had gone. So I got my father to drive me to your place. We'd have started sooner, but Cavalier got away. And we waited to look for him—to bring him along."

"Bring him along?" mutteringly echoed the blankbrained Link. "What fer?"

"Why," laughed the girl, "because your house is where he belongs and where he is going to live. Just as he has been living all summer."

Ferris caught his breath in a choked wheeze of unbelieving ecstasy.

"Gawd!" he breathed. "GAWD!"

Then, he stammered brokenly

"They—they don't seem no right words to—to thank you in, Ma'am. But maybe you und'stand what I'd want to say if I could?"

"Yes," she said gently. "I think I understand. I understood from the minute I saw you and the dog together. That's why I decided I didn't want him. That's why I—"

"An' you'll get that thousand dollars!" cried Link, his fingers buried rapturously in Chum's fur. "Ev'ry cent of it. I—"

"I think," interrupted the girl, winking very fast. "I think I've got what I wanted, already. My father doesn't want the money either. Do you, Dad?"

"Oh, for heaven's sake, stop rubbing it in!" fumed Gault. "Come on home! It's getting cold. I ought to thank the Lord for not having you anywhere near me in Wall Street, girl! You'd send me under the hammer in a week."

He kicked the accelerator, and the little car whizzed off in the twilight.

"Chum," observed Ferris, gaping after it. "Chum, I guess the good Lord built that gal the same day He built YOU. If He did—well, He sure done one grand day's work!"

CHAPTER IV.

The Choice

Luck had come at last to the Ferris farm. Link's cash went into improvements on the place, instead of going into the deteriorating of his inner man. And he worked the better. A sulky man is ever prone to be an inefficient man. And Link no longer sulked.

All this-combined with a wholesale boom in local agriculture, and especially in truck gardening—had wrought wonders in Link's farm and in Link's bank account. Within three years of Ferris's meeting with Chum the place's last mortgage was wiped out and a score of needed repairs and improvements were installed. Also the man had a small but steadily growing sum to his credit in a Paterson savings bank.

Life on the farm was mighty pleasant, nowadays. Work was hard, of course, but it was bringing results that made it more than worth while. Ferris and his dog were living on the fat of the land. And they were happy.

Then came the interruption that had been inevitable from the very first.

A taciturn and eternally dead-broke man, in a rural region, need not fear intrusion on his privacy. Convivial folk make detours round him, as if he were a mud puddle.

Thriftier and more respectable neighbors eye him askance or eye him not at all.

But when a meed of permanent success comes to such a man he need no longer be lonely unless he so wills. Which is not cynicism, but common sense. The convivial element will still fight shy of him. But he is welcomed into the circle of the respectable.

So it was with Link Ferris. Of old he had been known as a shiftless and harddrinking mountaineer with a sour farm that was plastered with mortgages. Now, he had cleared off his mortgages and had cleaned up his farm; and he and his home exuded an increasing prosperity.

People, meeting him in the nearby village of Hampton or at church, began to treat him with a consideration that the long-aloof farmer found bewildering.

Yet he liked it rather than not; being at heart a gregarious soul. And with gruff friendliness he met the advances of well-to-do neighbors who in old days had scarce favored him with a nod.

The gradual change from the isolated life of former years did not make any sort of a hit with Chum. The collie had been well content to wander through the day's work at his master's heels; to bring in the sheep and the cattle from pasture; to guard the farm from intruders—human or otherwise.

In the evenings it had been sweet to lounge at Link's feet, on the little white porch, in the summer dusk; or to lie in drowsy content in front of the glowing kitchen stove on icy nights when the gale screeched through the naked boughs of the dooryard trees and the snow scratched hungrily at the window panes.

Now, the dog's sensitive brain was aware of a subtle alteration. He did not object very much to the occasional visits at the house of other farmers and townsfolk during the erstwhile quiet evenings, although he had been happier in the years of peaceful seclusion.

But he grieved at his master's increasingly frequent absences from home. Nowadays, once or twice a week, Link was wont to dress himself in his best as soon as the day's work was done, and fare forth to Hampton for the evening.

Sometimes he let Chum go with him in these outings. Oftener of late he had said, as he started out:

"Not to-night, Chummie. Stay here."

Obediently the big dog would lay himself down with a sigh on the porch edge; his head between his white little forepaws; his sorrowful brown eyes following the progress of his master down the lane to the highroad.

But he grieved, as only a sensitive highbred dog can grieve—a dog who asks nothing better of life than permission to live and to die at the side of the man he has chosen as his god; to follow that god out into rain or chill; to starve with him, if need be; to suffer at his hands—in short, to do or to be anything except to be separated from him.

Link Ferris had gotten into the habit of leaving Chum alone at home, oftener and oftener of late, as his own evening absences from the farm grew more and more frequent.

He left Chum at home because She did not like dogs.

"She" was Dorcas Chatham, the daughter of Hampton's postmaster and general storekeeper.

Old Man Chatham in former days would have welcomed Cal Whitson, the official village souse, to his home as readily as he would have admitted the ne'er-do-well Link Ferris to that sanctuary. But of late he had noted the growing improvement in Link's fortunes, as evidenced by his larger store trade, his invariable cash payments and the frequent money orders which went in his name to the Paterson savings bank.

Wherefore, when Dorcas met Link at a church sociable and again on a straw ride and asked him to come and see her some time, her sire made no objection. Indeed he welcomed the bashful caller with something like an approach to cordiality.

Dorcas was a calm-eyed, efficient damsel, more than a little pretty, and with much repose of manner. Link Ferris, from the first, eyed her with a certain awe. When a mystic growing attraction was added to this and when it in turn merged into love, the sense of awe was not lost. Rather it was strengthened.

In all his thirty-one lean and lonely years Link had never before fallen in love. At the age when most youths are sighing over some wonder girl, he had been too busy fighting off bankruptcy and starvation to have time or thought for such things.

Wherefore, when love at last smote him it smote him hard. And it found him woefully unprepared for the battle.

He knew nothing of women. He did not know, for example, what the average youth finds out in his teens—that grave eyes and silent aloofness and lofty self-will and icy pietism in a maiden do not always signify that she is a saint and that she must be worshiped as such. Ferris had no one to tell him that far oftener these signs point merely to stupid narrowness and to lack of ideas.

Dorcas was clever at housework. She was quietly self-assured. She was good to look upon. She was not like any of the few girls Link had met. Wherefore he built for her a sacred shrine in his innermost heart; and he knelt before her image there.

If Ferris found her different from the other Hampton girls, Dorcas found him equally different from the local swains she knew. She recognized his hidden strength. The maternal element in her nature sympathized with his loneliness and with the marks it had left upon his soul.

For the rest—he was neither a village cut-up like Con Skerly, nor a solemn mass of conceit like Royal Crews; nor patronizing like young Lawyer Wetherell; nor vaguely repulsive like old Cap'n Baldy Todd, who came furtively a-courting her. Link was different. And she liked him. She liked him more and more.

Once her parents took Dorcas and her five-year-old sister, Olive, on a Sunday afternoon ramble, which led eventually to the Ferris farm. Link welcomed the chance callers gladly, and showed them over the place. Dorcas's housewifely eye rejoiced in the well-kept house, even while she frowned inwardly at its thousand signs of bachelor inefficiency. The stock and the crops, too, spoke of solid industry.

But she shrank back in sudden revolt as a huge tawny collie came bounding toward her from the fold where he had just marshaled the sheep for the night. The dog was beautiful. And he meant her no harm. He even tried shyly to make friends with the tall and grave-eyed guest. Dorcas saw all that. Yet she shrank from him with instinctive fear—in spite of it.

As a child she had been bitten—and bitten badly—by a nondescript mongrel that had been chased into the Chatham backyard by a crowd of stone-throwing boys, and which she had sought to oust with a stick from its hiding place under the steps. Since then Dorcas had had an unconquerable fear and dislike of dogs. The feeling was unconquerable because

95

she had made no effort to conquer it. She had henceforth judged all dogs by the one whose teeth marks had left a lifelong scar on her white forearm.

She had the good breeding not to let Ferris see her distaste for his pet that he was just then exhibiting so proudly to the guests. Her shrinking was imperceptible, even to a lover's solicitous eye. But Chum noted it. And with a collie's odd sixth sense he knew this intruder did not like him.

Not that her aversion troubled Chum at all; but it puzzled him. People as a rule were effusively eager to make friends with Chum. And—being ultraconservative, like the best type of collie—he found their handling and other attentions annoying. He had taken a liking to Dorcas, at sight. But since she did not return this liking Chum was well content to keep away from her.

He was the more content, because five-year-old Olive had flung herself, with loud squeals of rapture, bodily on the dog; and had clasped her fat little arms adoringly round his massive furry throat in an ecstasy of delight.

Chum had never before been brought into such close contact with a child. And Link watched with some slight perturbation the baby's onslaught. But in a moment Ferris's mind was at rest.

At first touch of the baby's fingers the collie had become once and for all Olive's slave. He fairly reveled in the discomfortingly tight caress. The tug of the little hands in his sensitive neck fur was bliss to him. Wiggling all over with happiness he sought to lick the chubby face pressed so tight against his ruff. From that instant Chum had a divided allegiance. His human god was Ferris. But this fluffy pink-and-white youngster was a mighty close second in his list of deities.

Dorcas looked on, trembling with fear; as her little sister romped with the adoring dog. And she heaved a sigh of relief when at last they were clear of the farm without mishap to the baby. For Olive had been dearer to Dorcas, from birth, than anyone or anything else on earth. To the baby sister alone Dorcas ceased to be the grave-eyed and self-assured Lady of Quality, and became a meek and worshiping devotee.

When Link Ferris at last mustered courage to ask Dorcas Chatham to marry him his form of proposal would have been ruled out of any novel or play. It consisted chiefly of a mouthful of half-swallowed, half-exploded words, spoken all in one panic breath, to the accompaniment of a mortal fear that shook him to the marrow.

Any other words, thus mouthed and gargled, would have required a full college of languages to translate them. But the speech was along a line perfectly familiar to every woman since Eve. And Dorcas understood. She would have understood had Link voiced his proposal in the Choctaw dialect instead of a slurringly mumbled travesty on English.

The man's stark earnestness of entreaty sent a queer flutter to the very depths of her calm soul. But the flutter failed to reach or to titillate the steady eyes. Nor did it creep into the level and self-possessed voice, as Dorcas made quiet answer:

"Yes. I like you better than any other man I know. And I'll marry you, if you're perfectly sure you care for me that way."

No, it was not the sort of reply Juliet made to the same question. It is more than doubtful that Cleopatra answered thus, when Antony offered to throw away the world for her sake. But it was a wholly correct and self-respecting response. And Dorcas had been rehearsing it for nearly a week.

Moreover, words are of use, merely as they affect their hearers. And all the passion poetry of men and of angels could not have thrilled Link Ferris as did Dorcas's correct and demure assent to his frenziedly gabbled plea. It went through the lovesick man's brain and heart like the breath of God.

And thus the couple became engaged.

With only a slight diminishing of his earlier fear did Link seek out Old Man Chatham to obtain his consent to the match. Dizzy with joy and relief he listened to that village worthy's ungracious assent also secretly rehearsed for some days.

For the best part of a month thereafter Link Ferris floated through a universe of roseate lights and soft music.

Then came the jar of awakening.

It was one Saturday evening, a week or so before the date set for the wedding. Dorcas broached a theme which had been much in her mind since the beginning of the engagement. She approached it very tactfully indeed, leading up to it in true feminine fashion by means of a cunningly devised series of levels which would have been the despair of a mining engineer. Having paved the way she remarked carelessly:

"John Iglehart was at the store to-day, father says. He's crazy about that big collie of yours."

Instantly Link was full of glad interest. It had been a sorrow to him that Dorcas did not like dogs. She had explained her dislike—purely on general principles—early in their acquaintance, and had told him of its origin. Link was certain she would come to love Chum, on intimate acquaintance. In the interim he did not seek to force her liking by bringing the collie to the Chatham house when he called.

Link did not believe in crossing a bridge until he came to it. There would be plenty of time for Dorcas to make friends with Chum in the long and happy days to come. Yet, now, he rejoiced that she herself should have been the first to broach the subject.

"Father says John is wild about Chum," went on the girl unconcernedly; adding, "By the way, John asked father to tell you he'd be glad to pay you $100 for the dog. It's a splendid offer, isn't it! Think of all the things we can get for the house with $100, Link! Why, it seems almost providential, doesn't it? Father says John is in earnest about it too. He—"

"In earnest, hey!" snapped Ferris, finding his voice after an instant of utter amazement. "In EARNEST! Well, that's real grand of him, ain't it! I'd be in earnest, too, if I was to bid ten cents for the best farm in Passaic County. But the feller who owned the farm wouldn't be in earnest. He'd be taking it as a fine joke. Like I do, when Johnny Iglehart has the nerve to offer $100 for a dog that wouldn't be worth a cent less'n $600—even if he was for sale. Why, that collie of mine—"

"If he is worth $600," suggested Dorcas icily, "you'd better not lose any time before you find someone who will pay that for him. He's no use to us. And $600 is too much money to carry on four legs. He—"

"No use to us?" echoed Link. "Why, Chum's worth the pay of a hired man to me, besides all the fondness I've got for him! He handles the sheep, and he—"

"So you've told me," interposed Dorcas with no show of interest. "I remember the first few times you came to see me you didn't talk of anything else, hardly, except that dog. Everybody says the same thing. It's a joke all through Hampton, the silly way you're forever singing his praises."

"Why shouldn't I?" demanded Link sturdily. "There's not a dandier, better pal anywhere, than what Chum's been to me. He—"

"Yes, yes," assented Dorcas, "I know. I don't doubt it. But, after all, he's only a dog, you know. And if you can get a good price for him, as you say, then the only thing to do is to sell him. In hard times like these—"

"Times ain't hard," denied Link tersely. "And Chum ain't for sale. That's all there is to it."

If one of her father's sleek cart horses had suddenly walked out of its stall with a shouted demand that it be allowed to do the driving, henceforth, and that its owners do the hauling, Dorcas Chatham could not have been much more surprised than at this unlooked-for speech from her humble suitor.

Up to now, Link Ferris had treated the girl as though he were unworthy to breathe the same air as herself. He had been pathetically eager to concede any and every mooted point to her, with a servile abasement which had roused her contempt, even while it had gratified her sense of power.

She had approached with tact the subject of Chum's disposal. But she had done so with a view to the saving of Link's feelings, not with the faintest idea that her love-bemused slave could venture to oppose her. She knew his fondness for the dog and she had not wished to bring matters to an issue, if tact would serve as well.

To punish her serf and to crush rebellion once and for all, as well as to be avenged for her wasted diplomacy, Dorcas cast aside her kindlier intent and drove straight to the point. Her calm temper was ruffled, and she spoke with a new heat:

"There is something you and I may as well settle, here and now, Link," she said. "It will save bickerings and misunderstandings, later on. I've told you how I hate dogs. They are savage and treacherous and—"

"Chum ain't!" declared Link stoutly.

"Why, that dog—"

"I hate dogs," she went on, "and I'm horribly afraid of them. I won't live in the same house with one. I don't want to hurt your feelings, Link, but you'll have to get rid of that great brown brute before you marry me. That is positive. So please let's say no more about it."

The man was staring at her with under jaw ajar. Her sharp air of finality grated on his every nerve. Her ultimatum concerning Chum left him dumfounded. But he forced himself to rally to the defense.

This glorious sweetheart of his did not understand dogs. He had hoped to teach her later to like and appreciate them. But apparently she must be taught at once that Chum could not be sold and that the collie must remain an honored member of the Ferris household. Marshaling his facts and his words, he said:

"I never told you about the time I was coming back home one night from the tavern here at Hampton, after I'd just cashed my pay check from the Pat'son market. I've never blabbed much about it, because I was drunk. Yes, it was back in them days. Just after I'd got Chum. A couple of fellers had got me drunk. And they set on me in a lonesome patch of the road by the lake; and they had me down and was taking the money away from me, when Chum sailed into them and druv them off. He had follered me, without me knowing. In the scrimmage I got tumbled headfirst into the lake. I was too drunk to get out, and my head was stuck in the mud, 'way under water. I'd 'a' drowned if Chum hadn't of pulled me out with his teeth in the shoulder of my coat. And that's the dog you're wanting me to sell?"

"You aren't likely to need such help again, I hope," countered the girl loftily, "now that you have stopped drinking and made a man of yourself. So Chum won't be needed for—"

"I stopped drinking," answered Link, "because I got to seeing how much more of a beast I was than the fine clean dog that was living with me. He made me feel 'shamed of myself. And he was such good comp'ny round the house that I didn't get lonesome enough to sneak down to the tavern all the time. It wasn't me that 'made a man of myself.' It was

Chum made a man of me. Maybe that sounds foolish to you. But—"

"It does," said Dorcas serenely. "Very foolish indeed. You don't seem to realize that a dog is only an animal. If you can get a nice home for the collie—such as John Iglehart will give him—"

"Iglehart!" raged Link, momentarily losing hold over himself. "If that mangy, wall-eyed slob comes slinking round my farm again, making friends with Chum, I'll sick the dog onto him; and have him run Iglehart all the way to his own shack! He's—! There! I didn't mean to cut loose like that!" he broke off at Dorcas's shudder of dismay. "Only it riles me something terrible to have him trying to get Chum away from me."

"There is no occasion to go losing your temper and shouting," reproved the girl. "Nothing is to be gained that way. Besides, that isn't the point. The point is this, since you force me to say it: You must get rid of that dog. And you must do it before you marry me. I won't set foot in your house until your dog is gone—and gone for good. I am sorry to speak so, but it had to be said."

She paused to give her slave a chance to wilt. But Link only sat, blank-faced, staring at her. His mind was in a muddle. All his narrow world was upside down. He couldn't make his brain grasp in full the situation.

All he could visualize for the instant was a shadowy mental image of Chum's expectant face; the tulip ears pricked forward, expectant; the jaws "laughing"; the deepset brown eyes abrim with gay affection and deathless loyalty for the man who was now asked to get rid of him. It didn't make sense. Half under his breath Link Ferris began to talk—or rather to ramble.

"There was one of the books over to the lib'ry," he heard himself meandering on, "with a queer story in it. I got to reading it through, one night last winter. It was about a feller named 'Fed'rigo.' A wop of some kind, I guess. He got so hard up he didn't have anything left but a pet falcon. Whatever a falcon may be. Whatever it was, it must'a been good to eat. But he set a heap of store by it. Him and it was chums. Same as me and Chum are. Then along come a lady he was in love with. And she stopped to his house for dinner. There wasn't anything in the house fit for her to eat. So he fed her the falcon. Killed the pet that was his chum, so's he could feed the dame he was stuck on. I thought, when I read it, that that feller was more kinds of a swine than I'd have time to tell you. But he wasn't any worse'n I'd be if I was to—"

"I'm sorry you care so little for me," intervened Dorcas, her voice very sweet and very cold, and her slender nose whitening a little at the corners of the nostrils. "Of course if you prefer a miserable dog to me, there's nothing more to be said. I—"

"No!" almost yelled the miserable man. "You've got me all wrong, dearie. Honest, you have. Can't you understand? Your little finger means a heap more to me than ev'rything else there is—except the rest of you—"

"And your dog," she supplemented.

"No!" he denied fiercely. "You got no right to say that! But Chum's served me faithful. And I can't kick him out like he was a—"

"Now you are getting angry again!" she accused, pale and furious. "I don't care to be howled at. The case stands like this: You must choose whether to get rid of that dog or to lose me. Take your choice. If—"

"I read in a story book about a feller that had a thing like that put up to him," said poor Link, unable to believe she was in earnest. "His girl said: 'You gotta choose between me and tobacco.' And he said: 'I'll choose tobacco. Not that I value tobacco so all-fired much,' he says, 'but because a girl, who'd make a man take such a choice, ain't worth giving up tobacco for.' You see, dearie, it's this way—"

"You'll have that dog out of your house and out of your possession, inside of twenty-four hours," she decreed, the white anger of a grave-eyed woman making her cold voice vibrate, "or you will drop my acquaintance. That is final.

And it's definite. The engagement is over—until I hear that your dog is killed or given away or sold. Good night!"

She left the room in vindictive haste. So overwhelmingly angry was she that she closed the door softly behind her, instead of slamming it. Through all his swirl of misery Link had sense enough to note this final symptom and wonder bitterly at it.

On his way out of the house he was hailed by a highpitched baby voice from somewhere above him. Olive had crawled out of bed, and in her white flannel pajamas she was leaning over the upper balustrade.

"Link!" she called down to the wretched man at the front door. "When you and Dorcas gets married together, I'm comin' to live wiv you! Then I can play wiv Chummie all I want to!"

Link bolted out to the street in the midst of her announcement. And, so occupied was he in trying to swallow a lump in his own throat, he failed to hear the sound of stifled sobbing from behind a locked door somewhere in the upper reaches of the house.

As the night wore on, the sleepless girl sought to comfort herself in the thought that Link had not definitely refused her terms. A night's reflection and an attitude of unbending aloofness on her own part might well bring him to a surrender.

Perhaps it was something in Link Ferris's dejected gait, as he turned into his own lane that night, perhaps it was the instinct which tells a collie when a loved human is unhappy—but Chum was at once aware of his master's woe. The dog, at first sound of Link's approaching steps, bounded from his vigil place on the porch and frisked joyously through the darkness to meet him. He sent forth a trumpeting bark of welcome as he ran.

Then—fifty feet from the oncoming man—the big collie halted and stood for an instant with ears cocked and eyes troubled. After which he resumed his advance; but at a solemn trot and with downcast mien. As he reached Link, the collie whined softly under his breath, gazing wistfully up into Ferris's face and then thrusting his cold nose lovingly into one of the man's loose-hanging hands.

Link had winced visibly at sound of the jubilantly welcoming bark. Now, noting the sudden change in the collie's demeanor, he stooped and caught the silken head between his hands. The gesture was rough, almost painful. Yet Chum knew it was a caress. And his drooping plume of a tail began to wag in response.

"Oh, CHUM!" exclaimed the man with something akin to a groan. "You know all about it, don't you, old friend? You know I'm the miser'blest man in North Jersey. You know it without me having to say a word. And you're doing your level best to comfort me. Just like you always do. You never get cranky; and you never say I gotta choose betwixt this and that; and you never get sore at me. You're just my chum. And you're fool enough to think I'm all right. Yet she says I gotta get rid of you!"

The dog pressed closer to him, still whining softly and licking the roughly caressing hands.

"What'm I going to do, Chummie?" demanded Link brokenly. "What'm I going to do about it? I s'pose any other feller'd call me a fool—like she thinks I am and tell me to sell you. If you was some dogs, that'd be all right. But not with YOU, Chum. Not with you. You'd mope and grieve for me, and you'd be wond'ring why I'd deserted you after all these years. And you'd get to pining and maybe go sick. And the feller that bought you wouldn't understand. And most likely he'd whale you for not being more chipper-like. And you haven't ever been hit. I'd—I'd a blame' sight sooner shoot you, than to let anyone else have you, to abuse you and let you be unhappy for me, Chum. A blame' sight rather."

Side by side they moved on into the darkened house. There, with the dog curled at his feet, Link Ferris lay broad awake until sunrise.

Early the next afternoon Dorcas decided she stood in need of brisk, outdoor exercise. Olive came running down the path after her, eagerly demanding to be taken along. Dorcas with much sternness bade her go back. She wanted to be alone, unless—But she refused to admit to herself that there was any "unless."

Olive, grievously disappointed, stood on the steps, watching her big sister set off up the road. She saw Dorcas take the righthand turn at the fork. The baby's face cleared. Now she knew in which direction Dorcas was going. That fork led to the Glen. And the Glen was a favorite Sunday afternoon ramble for Link and Chum. Olive knew that, because she and Dorcas more than once had walked thither to meet them.

Olive was pleasantly forgetful of her parents' positive command that she refrain from walking alone on the motor-infested Sunday roads. She set off at a fast jog trot over the nearby hill, on whose other side ran the Glen road.

Link Ferris, with Chum at his heels, was tramping moodily toward the Glen. As he turned into the road he paused in his sullen walk. There, strolling unconcernedly, some yards in front of him, was a tall girl in white. Her back was toward him. Yet he would have recognized her at a hundred times the distance. Chum knew her, too, for he wagged his tail and started at a faster trot to overtake her.

"Back!" called Link.

Purposely he spoke as low as possible. But the dog heard and obeyed. The girl, too, started a little, and made as if to turn. Just then ensued a wild crackling in the thick roadside bushes which lined the hillside from highway to crest. And a white-clad little bunch of humanity came galloping jubilantly out into the road, midway between Dorcas and Link.

At the road edge Olive's stubby toe caught in a noose of blackberry vine. As the youngster was running full tilt, her own impetus sent her rolling over and over into the center of the dusty turnpike.

Before she could get to her feet or even stop rolling, a touring car came round the bend, ten yards away—a car that was traveling at a speed of something like forty-five miles an hour, and whose four occupants were singing at the top of their lungs.

Link Ferris had scarce time to tense his muscles for a futile spring—Dorcas's scream of helpless terror was still unborn—when the car was upon the prostrate child.

And in the same fraction of a second a furry catapult launched itself across the wide road at a speed that made it look like tawny blur.

Chum's mad leap carried him to the baby just as the car's fender hung above her. A slashing grip of his teeth in the shoulder of her white dress and a lightning heave of his mighty neck and shoulders—and the little form was hurtling through the air and into the weed-filled wayside ditch.

In practically the same instant Chum's body whizzed into the air again. But this time by no impetus of its own. The high-powered car's fender had struck it fair, and had tossed it into the ditch as though the dog had been a heap of rags.

There—huddled and lifeless—sprawled the beautiful collie. The car put on an extra spurt of speed and disappeared round the next turn.

Olive was on her feet before Dorcas's flying steps could reach her. Unhurt but vastly indignant, the baby opened her mouth to make way for a series of howls. Then, her eye falling on the inert dog, she ran over to Chum and began to cry out to him to come to life again.

"No use of that, kid!" interposed Link, kneeling beside the collie he loved and smoothing the soiled and rumpled fur. "It's easier to drop out of life than what it is to come back to it again. Well," he went on harshly, turning to the weeping Dorcas, "the question has answered itself, you see. No need now to tell me to get rid of him. He's saved me the bother. Like he was always saving me bother. That being Chum's way."

Something in his throat impeded his fierce speech. And he bent over the dog again, his rough hands smoothing the pitifully still body with loving tenderness. Dorcas, weeping hysterically, fell on her knees beside Chum and put her arms about the huddled shape. She seemed to be trying to say something, her lips close to one of the furry little ears.

"No use!" broke in Ferris, his voice as grating as a file's. "He can't hear you now. No good to tell him you hate dogs;

or that you're glad you've saw the last of him. Even if he was alive, he wouldn't understand that. He'd never been spoke to that way."

"Don't! Oh, don't!" sobbed the girl. "Oh, I'm so—"

"If you're crying for Chum," went on the grating voice, "there's no need to. He was only just a dog. He didn't know any better but to get his life smashed out'n him, so somebody else could go on living. All he asked was to be with me and work for me and love me. After you said he couldn't keep on doing that, there ain't any good in your crying for him. It must be nice—if you'll only stop crying long enough to think of it—to know he's out of your way. And I'M out of it too!" he went on in a gust of fury. "S'pose you two just toddle on, now, and leave me to take him home. I got the right to that, anyhow."

He stooped to pick up the dog; and he winked with much rapidity to hold back an annoying mist which came between him and Chum. His mouth corners, too, were twitching in a way that shamed him. He had a babyish yearning to bury his face in his dead friend's fur, and cry.

"DON'T!" Dorcas was wailing. "Oh, you can't punish me any worse than I'm—"

Her sob-broken voice scaled high and swelled out into a cry of stark astonishment. Slowly Chum was lifting his splendid head and blinking stupidly about him!

113

The fender had smitten the collie just below the shoulder, in a mass of fur-armored muscles. In falling into the wayside ditch his skull had come into sharp contact with a rock. Knocked senseless by the concussion, he had lain as dead, for the best part of five minutes. After which he had come slowly to his senses—bewildered, bruised and sore, but otherwise no worse for the accident.

He came to himself to find a weeping woman clutching him stranglingly round the neck, while she tried to kiss his dust-smeared head.

Chum did not care at all for this treatment, especially from a comparative stranger. But he saw his adored master looking so idiotically happy—over that or something else—that the dog forbore to protest.

"If you really wanted him put out of the way so bad—" began Link, when he could trust himself to speak.

He got no further. Dorcas Chatham turned on him in genuine savageness. The big eyes were no longer grave and patronizing. The air of aloofness had fallen from the girl like a discarded garment.

"Link!" she blazed. "Link Ferris! If you ever dare speak about getting rid of—of MY dog,—I'll—I'll never speak to you again, as long as—as long as we're married!"